Akash shook her hand ~~~~ they had never met before. As if not just two nights ago they hadn't been entwined in each other's bodies in the same bed.

As if touching her hand had no effect on him whatsoever. "Nice to finally meet you, Ms. Pandya. I have heard a lot about you from your father."

Reena gave a curt nod as she pulled her hand free of the strength and warmth of his. He should get an Oscar. He showed zero signs of knowing her. "I can't say I've heard anything of you. So you have me at a disadvantage, as my father has yet to tell me the deal he struck with you."

Her father cleared his throat. "Mr. Gupta insisted we keep this a surprise."

Reena raised an eyebrow at her father.

Akash spoke as they walked to the table. "I understand that Lulu's is having financial difficulties. Unable to make the bank payments, struggling to meet operating costs." He had the audacity to fix her in his gaze.

"That is true." Reena met his eyes, masking her expression as she had so many times. "I had something to help, but it has fallen through."

Dear Reader,

Welcome to book four in the Once Upon a Wedding series! I am so excited that you picked up *The Business Between Them*! I've never written the enemies-to-lovers trope, but when Reena popped into my head as the badass person running Lulu's Boutique Hotel, I knew I was going to try. Though, of course, I put a twist on it.

Reena Pandya and Akash Gupta have a Vegas fling and fall in love, to their mutual surprise, and they decide to keep their relationship secret while they figure out where it's going. Before they can figure that out, Reena hides the fact that Akash's sister's fiancé is cheating on her so that Lulu's will still have that wedding.

Akash is furious and breaks up with Reena, but he is already committed to the deal he made with her father, to give Lulu's money so it doesn't go under. Of course, Reena is unhappy about this!

Follow Reena and Akash as they traverse having to work together when they are no longer together but might still be having feelings they need to address. Of course, there's a wedding and food—and you may meet some old friends here as well!

I'd love to connect with you! You can find me on Facebook at Mona Shroff, Author; Instagram, @monashroffauthor; Twitter, @monashroffwrite; and TikTok, @monaseesandwrites. My website is monadshroff.com. I post about writing; reading; my dog, Nala—and my daughter's upcoming nuptials!

Thanks so much for reading! Enjoy!

Mona Shroff

The Business Between Them

MONA SHROFF

HARLEQUIN
SPECIAL
EDITION

HARLEQUIN®

**SPECIAL
EDITION**™

Recycling programs
for this product may
not exist in your area.

ISBN-13: 978-1-335-72478-6

The Business Between Them

For questions and comments about the quality of this book,
please contact us at CustomerService@Harlequin.com.

Harlequin Enterprises ULC
22 Adelaide St. West, 41st Floor
Toronto, Ontario M5H 4E3, Canada
www.Harlequin.com

Printed in U.S.A.

Mona Shroff has always been obsessed with everything romantic, so it's fitting that she writes romantic stories by night, even though she's an optometrist by day. If she's not writing, she's likely to be making melt-in-your-mouth chocolate truffles, reading, or raising a glass of her favorite gin and tonic with friends and family. She's blessed with an amazing daughter and a loving son, who have both left the nest! Mona lives in Maryland with her romance-loving husband and their rescue dog, Nala.

Books by Mona Shroff

Harlequin Special Edition

Once Upon a Wedding

The Five-Day Reunion
Matched by Masala
No Rings Attached

Visit the Author Profile page
at Harlequin.com for more titles.

To Hetal and Tina,
for always having my back like sisters do.

Acknowledgments

Every book I write is a challenge, but this book was a struggle, as sometimes they are. I am forever grateful to my village of support, who listen as I moan and groan, and who help me out by listening and offering sage advice as well as insight into the book itself. Shaila Patel, Farah Heron, Namrata Patel, Nisha Sharma and Angelina M. Lopez—you ladies are the absolute best!

To my dear bestie, Kosha Dalal, who guided me through equity and angel investors and the practicality of Akash and Reena's financial deals— thank you, thank you! Your guidance helped pave the way for this story.

My editor, Susan Litman, who always has wonderful things to say before she helps me improve my book in every way—thank you for your faith in me! Rachel Brooks, my agent of five years (and counting!), I love knowing that you are behind me in every way.

To my family and friends, as always your support and understanding when I need to be writing makes writing easier.

And, as always, Deven, I couldn't have done any of this without you.

Prologue

Reena Pandya entered the apartment, took off her heels and suit jacket, placing them neatly in the closet. Tears that she had kept at bay for hours burned behind her eyes.

She had failed.

She'd done everything in her power to save her family legacy, Lulu's Boutique Hotel, to no avail. Her heart was broken.

Technically, Lulu's belonged to her parents. But between her and her two brothers, she was the one who wanted to run the family business. She was the one who was to have been the owner.

But not after tonight. After tonight, the bank would own Lulu's. Tears started to pool, causing her vision to blur. It didn't matter, really. After six months, she could navigate Akash Gupta's giant loft blindfolded. Falling for Akash was the one thing in her life she hadn't planned on, but his love had become the one thing she had come to rely on.

She walked down the small hallway to the large sitting room. Right now, she simply needed the strength and warmth of Akash's arms around her, so she could forget the world for a little while. She didn't want to think about how she had failed her family, or worse how she had failed herself. Getting lost in Akash's support and faith would give her the strength to face tomorrow.

Because tomorrow, the hotel that meant so much to her, that she'd fought so hard for, would be lost. A thought she could hardly bear. And tomorrow was also her twenty-seventh birthday. The day that her father was supposed to transfer Lulu's to her.

The scent of Akash's cologne wafted softly in the air. He was home. The thought calmed her ache.

His sister, Asha Gupta, was an upcoming social media influencer. She'd booked her wedding at Lulu's, and the event would have been just the thing to help bring major revenue—and media attention—to her floundering hotel. But Asha's fiancé had been caught cheating on her, which meant no wedding. No money. No media.

Which meant that unless the mortgage money showed up by some miracle, Reena was losing her family's business tomorrow.

Although not for her lack of trying to cover up Asha's fiancé's—well, her *ex*-fiancé's— indiscretions.

Reena had only known for just the past twenty-four hours, but yes. She'd been willing to cover it up and allow the wedding to proceed anyway. She ran a hotel. A business. Not a clinic for relationship troubles.

They were behind in operating expense payments, and the bank note was a week overdue. There simply was not any money. Or time. She'd simply had no other options. That's why Akash was waiting for her. Because he knew she'd come here.

He'd clearly been angry about the way she had handled the wedding cancellation. She had seen the pain and anger in his movements when he left the restaurant. Of course he was upset, but once she had a chance to explain, she was sure he would understand.

Their bond had only been deepening these past few months—it was something she had come to rely on. She craved that constant now more than ever.

She stepped into the living room, where the only light came from a small table lamp. Akash must have heard her come in, but he said nothing as he stood, facing out toward the floor to ceiling windows, taking in the night view of Inner Harbor. Lights reflected in the water from waterfront restaurants, the silhouttes of the tall ships in the distance. He raised his glass of bourbon to his lips and sipped.

"Hey." Reena walked toward him. "I was hoping to find you here." She wrapped her arms around him from his back as she had done so many times over the past few months. She loved holding him like this, where she could feel his body flush with hers. Where she could feel the strength in his back and revel in the comfort of his scent. But instead of relaxing into her embrace as he usually did or turning around and enveloping her in his arms, his muscles tensed.

"What's the matter?" She pulled back.

"You're kidding, right?" Akash's voice was a low grumble on a regular day. Right now, laced with anger as it was, it was a whisper, a rumble deep in his throat.

Even in a bad mood, it was sexy as hell.

"I'm sorry?" She walked around so she was facing him. That's when she saw the anguish in his eyes.

"What happened?"

She furrowed her brow. He had been there. He had heard. "Rahul cheated on your sister."

Her pressed his lips together, narrowing his eyes at her as if she were being flippant. "I got that. What I don't get is that fact that you knew about it."

She opened her mouth to explain, but he cut her off.

"How could you?" he spat the words at her with venom. "This was supposed to be a…a mutually beneficial arrangement, Reena. I wanted my sister's wedding to be held at Lulu's so you could get to know her without revealing who we are to each other. So that when we decided to let our families know we were together, it wouldn't be a complete shock." He paused for breath. "And so you could save Lulu's." He took a step away from her, shaking his head. "But then you were ready to let her marry a cheater." The words hit her like knives.

Reena fought to maintain her composure. It was a skill she had refined over years being in the hotel business. Never let them see you sweat. "She's a client. It's my responsibility to remain detached, to be professional. Private matters between my clients are private."

Akash's eyes widened in disbelief. Reena raised an eyebrow at him. As if he had never put business before emotion before. "Your job is the definition of putting business before people—"

"She's my *sister*. My family," Akash said. "Doesn't that mean anything to you?" He did not wait for her reply. "Business isn't everything."

Reena clamped her mouth shut. Six months together. The things they'd shared together. The things they'd done. The things they'd said to one another behind closed doors.

Things like *I love you*.

All reduced to his last words. Her heart thudded in her already drained body, the pounding reverberating in her ears.

"Lulu's is more than a business. It's my family legacy. Everything I did was to save that legacy. Everything my parents worked and sacrificed for." She paused for breath. Her frustration fumed inside her.

"She's my sister—but even without that, she's a person. A person who does not deserve to be married to a known cheater, just so you can use their wedding to save your hotel." Akash didn't yell when he was angry. He seethed.

"You know what? This is over." His gravelly tone cracked a bit on the last word. "I watched your cutthroat attitude in business dealings before, but I never thought you would stoop this low." He continued.

Her heart throbbed in her chest. *This low?* Was he

serious right now? She had seen his father rob hundreds of people of their jobs as he bought and sold businesses. Health care stripped, retirements lost. Near complete disregard for actual people and their lives. Akash himself had pushed through a few deals like that personally. He'd come to her, in those times, heartbroken that people had lost their jobs. But he'd done the deals anyway. It was *business*.

"You made your choice, when you erased the video of Rahul kissing another woman. The evidence of his cheating." Akash tossed back the remains of the whiskey in his glass.

He smelled amazing, the musky remnants of his cologne, leather from his jacket, and him. She had gotten used to that scent at the end of the day—no matter how long the day had been—had even found it comforting.

She ripped herself away from him and the comfort that he had once offered. She had been trying to save her family's legacy. Their hotel. She had to save it; it was everything to her. Akash knew this.

Akash stared at her and shook his head. "I… I thought I knew who I fell in love with." He hardened his gaze. "Clearly I did not."

Reena stared him down, pushing back those tears and ignoring the light-headed feeling of her world falling apart. Her world crashed and folded as she turned back toward the door. Mechanically, she slipped on her heels and grabbed her jacket. This couldn't be happening.

Except that it was.

She fought the tears and screams of anguish and

frustration that were building up inside her. She wouldn't give him the satisfaction. She spoke through gritted teeth. "Neither did I."

Chapter One

Six Weeks Later

It was midmorning when Reena arrived at what was supposed to have been her office, but was still her father's office. Though in truth, neither of them should still be here, since there hadn't been any money to pay the bank six weeks ago. Her father had been very vague about the whole thing, but apparently, someone had stepped in and paid the mortgage for one month. She had done everything short of go through his files to find out what had happened, to no avail. Her resume stood ready in her computer, but her father had insisted that she not send it out, that he 'had something in the works'.

She abided by his wishes, but every day was a small

torture. She couldn't bear to face him. She'd failed, and now another month had passed, another payment was due at the bank, but as far as she knew, they had nothing.

The hotel would never be hers. She should just send out her resumé.

If the bank took possession, they'd sell the hotel to someone. The thought of Lulu's belonging to some chain entity brought the burn of tears to her eyes. She'd practically grown up in Lulu's. The hotel was where she and her brothers came after school. As they got older, they all worked in the hotel in some capacity. For as long as she could remember, Reena had wanted nothing more than to run Lulu's. Her older brother Sonny became a chef, and now had his own restaurant, The Masala Hut; her younger brother Jai was still in college. As far as she knew, her brothers had other dreams that they would pursue. If she didn't take over Lulu's, her parents would simply sell it.

It was unthinkable.

Reena aquired her business degree as well as her degree in hospitality, all with the sole focus of taking over the family business. When it had been failing, she had convinced her brother, Sonny, to fake a relationship with a wedding planner just so she could secure Asha Gupta's wedding.

That had backfired in so many ways that she was still picking up the pieces.

She swallowed back the emotion that threatened to spill.

Her father had called early that morning and asked

for this meeting, saying he had set something up. Something that would ensure that the bank did not get Lulu's.

It had also been six weeks since Akash had left her. She would have thought that she would be done crying about it by now, but no such luck. Between losing the man she'd loved and the job she lived for, tears wet her pillow every night as peaceful sleep eluded her.

Falling in love had never been a priority for her. She knew she was not willing to sacrifice the hotel for anyone or anything. Anyone who was going to be in her life in any capacity was going to have to be okay with that.

Not that she had envisioned her life without a partner. How could she when she saw her parents almost every day? They were the ultimate team, working side by side. She had mentioned them to Akash many times as the gold standard of relationships. Something to strive for, something to achieve. He had seemed impressed, eager to meet them. Maybe because his own parents had divorced when he was young.

She had opted to go to her dojo each night and spar the heavy bag for an hour. She'd leave exhausted and spent, but still heartbroken. After a quick shower, she'd opened her laptop to work.

She glanced at her bandaged knuckles. She knew better than to spar without protection, but the last few nights, she hadn't cared. She'd wanted to feel the bag with her knuckles, disregarding when they'd bled.

Sleep was elusive, and she'd woken up tired and with swollen eyes. She went for her run, choosing a route that did not go past The Masala Hut. When she got back home, she showered and dressed and did the best she could to cover up her exhausted expression with coffee and makeup.

She glanced down at her lime-colored pantsuit, smoothed her ponytail and lifted her chin. On an inhale, her armor clicked into place and she pushed open the door. "Papa. Good morning." She paused for a moment as she realized her mother was here, too. Reena's muscles tensed. She didn't know why; it was just always that way with her mother. They both handled the day-to-day operations of Lulu's, her mother less so lately as Reena took on more. "Mom."

Her father looked up from his computer where she knew he was reading the paper. "Beti." There was affection in his voice. "Jai Shree Krishna."

"Jai Shree Krishna." Her mother said as well, Reena was convinced that the hint of affection in her mother's voice was drowned out by disappointment.

"I spoke with your brother this morning," her father said as he returned to his desk.

"Yeah?"

"Restaurant is doing well." He grinned at Reena.

"Glad to hear it." And she was. Sonny deserved success and happiness. She paused. "What is this solution that you have come up with?"

Her father's secretary buzzed at that moment. "Mr. Pandya. Mrs. Pandya. He is here."

He gave her tight smile. "He's here." Her mother nodded at her father, but Reena could feel the waves of accusation flowing from her. Her mother hardly made eye contact with her. Of course it was because Reena had failed at keeping Lulu's in the family.

Reena turned her back to the door to look out the window. She had always loved this view. She could see the whole harbor from here, as well as the city. It was calming. She would need this moment before she could face whatever was ahead for Lulu's. The most likely scenario was that the bank would take it over, and once they had it, she'd never have a chance to get it back. Her heart went heavy in her chest, and tears prickled at her nose at just the thought. She inhaled deeply and exhaled slowly, regaining her control over her emotions, reinstating her armor.

A knock at the door behind her had her straightening her back.

"Come in." Her father's voice commanded. It was reassuring to hear the authority in his voice. As if he was still in charge.

The door opened and Reena continued to look out the window, unable to face what was behind her. Every second she faced the water was an extra second that her dreams were still hers.

Her father's chair swooshed on the carpet as he stood. "Mr. Gupta. Thank you for meeting so early."

"Mr. Pandya. Mrs. Pandya."

At the sound of that voice, that familiar low rumble, Reena's entire body sparked to life as if hit by lightning.

It can't be.

There was no way.

"Please, call me Harish." Her father chuckled.

Her mother offered no such lenience. "Mr. Gupta," she said.

"Call me Akash." His tone was friendly, but businesslike.

Reena closed her eyes. The world spun. Her heart raced and she was vaguely faint.

What the hell was he doing here?

There was no possible way that the man whose touch she had melted into time and time again—the man who *dumped* her—could possibly have a role in her father's grand plan to save the business. It was too much, a slap in the face from a universe that seemed to use her life as a comedy show.

Without opening her eyes, she knew exactly where Akash was standing. She couldn't feel him, she was just heartbreakingly *aware of him. Six weeks later and she was still just. So. Aware of him. Of his presence. To have him this close to her, with her parents in the room was sheer torture, because regardless of the anger that had passed between them, her body still responded to his...*

But none of that mattered, not now. Akash Gupta could only be here to buy the hotel. He worked for his father's investment company, Gupta Equity. Pradeep Gupta basically bought struggling businesses and then sold them for parts, with little to no thought for the people who worked in those companies, or their lives.

Well, over her dead body was Gupta Equity going to get this hotel.

She masked her expression and spun around, her hand extended. "Mr. Gupta. Reena Pandya."

Akash shook her hand and nodded as if they had never met before. As if not just a month and a half ago they hadn't been entwined in each other's bodies in the same bed. As if touching her hand had no effect on him whatsoever, when her body had questioned why they were only touching hands as opposed to melting into one another.

"Nice to finally meet you, Ms. Pandya. I've heard a great deal about you from your father."

Reena gave a curt nod as she pulled her hand free of the strength and warmth of his. He should get an Oscar. He showed zero signs of knowing her. Or maybe he truly was not affected. Because maybe he really didn't care. "I can't say I've heard anything of you. So you have me at a disadvantage, as my parents have yet to tell me the deal they struck with you."

Her father cleared his throat. "Mr. Gupta insisted we keep this a surprise."

Reena raised an eyebrow at her father, forcing herself to remain calm. Did he?

Akash spoke as they walked to the table. "I understand that Lulu's is having financial difficulties. Unable to make the bank payments, struggling to meet operating costs." He had the audacity to fix her in his gaze.

"That is true." Reena met his eyes, masking her expression as she had so many times. "I had something in mind to help, but it has fallen through."

"Oh." Her mother looked at her. "Mr. Gupta is well aware of what happened. Asha Gupta is his sister." She cleared her throat.

What Reena had to mask here was not the sibling

relationship of which she already knew, but the fact that her parents knew of it, as well as the fact that they knew about what she had been ready to do to Asha.

"It is a shame that your sister's fiancé turned out to be unfaithful. How fortunate that my brother found out." Reena kept her voice clinical. Another skill she had acquired at her mother's knee.

"She's tough. She'll survive." Akash shot her a heated glance, the only action so far that indicated they had any history at all. It was gone in a millisecond.

"I have no doubt." Reena remained blank. "Now about the deal." She looked expectantly from her parents to Akash. The fact that they were bothering with this small talk told her that her parents were wary of her reaction. "Just lay it out." She fixed her gaze on Akash. "I'm pretty tough, too."

"Very well. Ms. Pandya. Gupta Equity is giving Lulu's a lump sum to be used for operating expenses as well as paying your bank note." Akash spoke to her with a voice she'd never heard before. It was most definitely the voice he used when he was breaking people's hearts.

Nausea began to claw at Reena. Gupta Equity would not do this just to be nice. They wanted something. She maintained her calm exterior. "In exchange for…"

Akash lifted his chin and fixed her in his gaze, his beautiful jaw set. "Fifty-one percent of Lulu's Boutique Hotel."

Her father snapped his head to Akash, but her mother spoke first. "Fifty-one percent? We have been negotiating for a few months and we had agreed on forty-nine percent."

Akash fixed his gaze on her mother. "Yes. Well." He flicked dark brooding eyes on Reena, and then back to her mother. "Things…have changed."

They had been negotiating for months? Son of a bitch. All those discussions she'd had with Akash about how she was trying to save the hotel, how it was her family legacy. All the things she had been trying to do for the hotel; getting a new chef for the restaurant, a new look for the hotel that reflected their culture, endless days and nights going over the books, trying to find a way to cut costs –had her parents seen none of that? Had they not noticed how all she had ever wanted or dreamed of was owning and running this hotel. She had even hired a new young and eager intern who had a fabulous plan for helping with her staffing issues.

Reena had shared all of this with Akash, how things might be looking up. And all along, he was negotiating a deal with her parents to buy it?

Screw him. And his giant stupid white horse. She hadn't asked him to save her. She could save herself just fine. She ignored the very idea that they were sitting here meant that she in fact, had not done so.

Her heart thudded, the sound loud in her ears.

"Ms. Pandya? Did you hear me?" Akash was watching her with dark eyes.

"Excuse me?"

"I said, as fifty-one percent owner of a business in decline, it is our job to find out what's not working and fix it. I hope we can count on your cooperation."

"I need to be able to buy it back," she stated.

"What?" Akash shot at her, his mask dropping for an instant and she saw the anger he was keeping hidden, before he hid it again.

She also registered her mother swing her head to her, but Reena could only deal with one failure at a time.

"You will give me first option at buying the hotel back, before you try to sell it to whatever chain will fill your pockets." She threw out her words with such disdain there was no doubt as to what she thought of his pockets.

"That is highly irregular."

"I know how it works. Irregular does not mean impossible. I'm sure you can make it happen."

"You are in no position to make demands." Akash growled revealing his irritation.

She allowed satisfaction to show on her face. "Aren't I? If you refuse, the bank will take over—"

"Ensuring that you never get it back."

"Gupta Equity holding fifty-one percent is the same thing to me," she spat out at him, her eyes lasered on him. "I get first option by one year from today, or no deal." She sat back and feigned typing something into her phone. "I can wait if you need to call your dad."

This was the problem and the pleasure with having been intimate with someone. Akash Gupta wanted to be his own man. Yet, he had come to work for his father, just to get a start, and five years later he was still there. When Akash dreamed, he dreamed of leaving

Gupta Equity, of getting out from under his father. And Reena knew it.

"I do not need to call anyone." Akash leaned forward, a smirk on his face. "This is my deal." He paused. "Fine. You have first option. But only if our changes work, and Lulu's is profitable by then."

She held out her hand, her ice queen face in place. "Deal."

Chapter Two

Akash shook Reena's hand, being careful not to hold on too long, or to get caught up in the warmth and familiarity of her touch. He had been prepared for the first handshake, but this one had taken him by surprise. The less he touched her, the better.

Their lawyers joined them and they went through the technicality of signing papers—Mr. Pandya had insisted on actual paper, not quite trusting digital signatures.

Harish Pandya's secretary buzzed him with an urgent call, and he and Mrs. Pandya excused themselves. "Sorry, Mr. Gupta. Please help yourself to coffee or chai." He nodded at the coffee service at the other end of his office, "We'll pick up in just a minute."

Akash sat across from her. She was ramrod straight,

her hair and makeup were perfect, polished, and her focus seemed singular.

She showed no signs of emotion, nothing that gave away a hint of their connection to each other—or that they even knew each other at all, for that matter. She had brought the ice queen to work today.

That was fine. After all, they were finished. His own insides were in agony, though. True, he was the one who had broken it off, but that did not mean he hadn't loved her. No matter how hard he tried to convince himself otherwise. He simply should have known better, and protected his heart.

He should have known that loving someone only ended in anguish.

"A couple months?" she said, finally turning her gaze to him.

"I'm sorry?"

"You were talking to my father about 'saving' Lulu's with your money for a couple months?" Her words were clipped. "While we were still 'together'?" She used air quotes around *together*, and Akash felt it as a stab to his already pained heart.

He opened his mouth to retort, but she continued, her eyes blazing. "A couple months during which I was confiding in you all the plans I had for saving Lulu's." She raised her voice.

"I was—"

"You were going to throw money at Lulu's because you didn't think that I would be able to save it. You did not believe in me." She shook her head, disgusted at him.

"That's not—"

"You lied. You told me night after night how you believed in me, how you knew I would save Lulu's." There were tears in her eyes, but her voice was steady. "How you loved me for it." She paused. "I have news for you. I could have saved Lulu's—"

"At my sister's expense," Akash barked at her.

"I do not have to explain myself to you." Reena sat back from where she had been leaning toward him.

"I do not have to explain myself to you, either," Akash growled at her.

She shook her head. "I honestly don't even know who you are anymore. It's as if we're meeting for the first time."

"We are," Akash said, meeting her gaze. He certainly had never seen this part of her before. The part that was willing to sacrifice people for her own benefit. It was not completely consistent with the woman he had fallen in love with.

But it was not inconsistent with the sharp business person he knew her to be.

"Sorry about that." Harish and Jaya Pandya reentered the room. "Let's take a look, shall we?"

"I'm happy to look it over, Papa," Reena offered.

Her father grinned at her. "You'll have plenty of documents to look over after we sign this agreement."

Reena glanced at Akash. He remained blank.

"Your mother and I are taking time away from Lulu's. After today, all decisions will be yours. You'll have Lulu's. Like you always wanted."

Reena pursed her lips and Akash saw the fury and

sadness in her face and eyes. "I'll have forty-nine per-cent." Her voice was bland, clinical. Not the warm energy Akash was used to. Had been used to.

"Yes, well… Beti…"

"Don't, Papa. I get it. I had a chance to save Lulu's and I…did not. So I get forty-nine percent."

It was killing her, not to have all of Lulu's, Akash knew it. For a moment, he felt her pain, and not because he found himself in a similar situation with his own father, but because he knew how much Lulu's meant to her, and not having full control would lie heavy in her heart.

Mr. Pandya turned to Akash. "If there's nothing else…"

Akash could walk out now. He could leave Lulu's to Reena and her family.

But then the bank would take it, and they would all lose. This was business. It wasn't personal. Isn't that what Reena had said when she had been willing to let Asha marry a cheater?

Not to mention this deal was the first big step on his way away from his father's company.

Akash signed the last document and stood. "No. We're all set." He offered his hand to them all. Mr. and Mrs. Pandya each shook it. Reena hesitated a moment before she too shook his hand. He should have withdrawn it. This was the third time in an hour that he'd had to touch her. Her shake was firm and brief. She dropped his hand almost instantly. "I'll be in touch."

Reena nearly stomped out the door—he flinched though it shut with the softest of clicks. He willed himself not to go after her, to simply smile and control his breathing as he wrapped up with her parents.

If he didn't, he'd chase after her.

After all, she'd taken his heart with her.

But there was no way he should be chasing after her. Not after the way she was willing to use his sister for her own purposes.

He'd made a mistake falling for her. It had been too fast. Too reckless. Too many nights of just sex and no sleep. And at the end of it all, they were just too damn different to make sense together.

That's what it was. He was just thinking with the wrong head.

And yet…even though he had spent the last six weeks insisting to himself that they were all wrong for each other—that *she* was all wrong for *him*—things just seemed to make more sense when he was with Reena. Even if. She. Was. Impossible.

Had he tricked himself into believing that maybe she was the one? No. He wasn't a fool. He knew that if there had ever been a woman that he could be with forever, it would have been Reena Pandya. He knew this was true, because why else would his heart be breaking right now?

Maybe he should have seen the red flag when she had wanted to keep their relationship a secret. But he hadn't wanted to share this new and wonderful thing with anyone else either. Neither of them had ever really prioritized a relationship, but they had started to without even really talking about it.

* * *

Akash dictated his directions to his assistant, Gemma, as he left Lulu's offices and headed into the waiting car. His stomach was in knots from Reena's touch. From having to be in her presence when she was no longer his. Even her perfume was torture. But her demeanor kept him in check—she appeared remorseless about her actions against his sister. All she cared about was Lulu's.

The car dropped him off at the office in the middle of a summer downpour. Fortunately, he only had a few feet to run before he was under the canopy of the building.

Gemma met him in the lobby with a small towel. They rode the elevator to his father's office while he dried his face and hair with the towel. "I'll need a few people with me to go over the books as well as inspect Lulu's. Sooner the better."

"I can round up people by tomorrow." Gemma was looking at her iPad.

"Perfect. You're the best, Gemma. Thank you."

She nodded and went to her office.

Akash went to his father's office for their daily business briefing.

"That's fine, Matt. Just get it done." His father was finishing up a call and nodded to Akash.

Akash helped himself to coffee and took a seat.

"How did it go?" His father asked. No *good morning, how are you, son?*—just down to business.

"As well as can be expected." Akash said as he took his seat across from his father's desk.

"Meaning?" His father sat down in front of his computer and started typing. Akash was used to this. It was rare that his father gave his attention to only one thing at a time.

"Meaning they negotiated a first option when we're ready to sell." He sipped his coffee.

"When *you're* ready to sell, you mean."

Akash nodded. "Of course." This was his deal. His father had made that much clear.

His father grinned. "I am excited to see you branching out like this. Gupta Equity will be far reaching."

"It's not Gupta, Dad. It's—"

His father waved a hand. "I know. It's AG Investments, all you. The thing is that this is not how you do business. Hotels are great, but they're not what Gupta does."

"No, Dad. But it is what *I* do. It's what AG does."

"You gave them first option." He shook his head, disbelieving. "As long as it's profitable. That means even if it's a small profit, you need to take it. You won't be able to shop it around."

"Dad, I have a plan. Just have some faith."

His father waved a hand at him as his assistant entered. "You ever going to tell me where you got the money for this?" He held up a hand to Matt and looked at Akash.

"It's all good, Dad." Akash shook his head. His dad would find out soon enough how he had paid for all this. No need to go into it now.

Putting money into Lulu's had seemed like a great idea at the time. Reena was slowly changing the decor and feel of Lulu's from a formal hotel to something more cozy, more home-away-from-home. She recognized that people traveled for work more than ever, and that they longed for the comforts of home, albeit in a luxurious manner. She was looking for a new chef to fill that sort of menu. She wanted a family feel for all her guests.

Lulu's simply needed an influx of cash. So a few months ago, Akash had approached Harish Pandya about this deal. It seemed win-win at the time. Reena got much needed cash, and he would finally be able to start on his own path away from his father.

His father pressed his mouth into a line. "Just don't forget the bottom line."

That was it right there. His dad was always about the bottom line. No matter who got hurt along the way.

The sooner Akash was free of Gupta Equity, the better.

Chapter Three

Two days after the sale went final, Reena was going over her staff schedule, when her assistant James came in. James was her age, taller than her, and always dressed to perfection in a suit and tie. Even at a young age, James exuded the right amount of propriety mixed with sarcasm, laced with fun.

"What?" She looked up at him and wondered if he'd be interested in being trained as front desk staff. She could really use someone there.

"Mr. Gupta has sent…people." He narrowed his blue eyes to show his distaste for this.

She stood, on instant alert; adrenaline pumped through her body. "He's what?"

"I need my accountant and lawyers to have access to your books." Akash stood in the doorway, magnificent in a blue suit that was clearly tailored to fit every muscle. His tie today was the same color as the suit, his shirt a crisp white. She told herself not to look at the pants, but she couldn't tear her gaze away. He was in beautifully fitted pants that matched perfectly. The shade of blue did amazing things for his skin. She recalled telling him that at one point. It was her favorite color, and she had gifted him that tie. There was only one reason he was wearing it now.

To irk her.

Akash stepped into the office, his hands in his pockets as James spun around. "Mr. Gupta." James took a step toward him. "This is highly irregular. Ms. Pandya's office is off-limits to—"

"Other people," Akash stated. "*I* can go where I want."

Reena glared at him. What a complete jerk. How had she ever thought she loved him? "It's okay, James." Reena's voice was gentle to James, but she had hardened her face at Akash. "I will deal with Mr. Gupta."

James eyed Akash with open trepidation and distrust. Clearly his sense of propriety did not extend to people who took over the business. "If you're sure."

Reena nodded at her assistant. "I am."

James left. But not before throwing Akash a look of complete disapproval. Reena had to smile to herself.

"What are you doing here?" she snapped, sitting back down, and continuing to type into her computer. She was typing nonsense, but he didn't know that. "I would think you had better things to do."

"Nope. Lulu's is my entire focus right now. I will

need my accountants to have access to your books," Akash stated as if he were talking to his secretary.

"That could have dealt with by email. My staff would have been happy to comply with the demands of the agreement." she retorted, deigning to glance at him. Mistake. Big mistake. There really was nothing hotter than Akash Gupta wearing a suit. Except maybe Akash Gupta *not* wearing a suit.

Stop!

"Possibly." He came closer until he was in front of her desk, close enough that she was enveloped in his scent. Cologne and soap, fresh from a shower. "But I like to see things for myself. I need to know what's going on here, so we can fix it."

Reena was livid. "You can't just barge in here without notice."

"Fifty-one percent says I can."

Reena seethed. "James." She called out. If she knew James—and after four years together, she did—he was just outside the door listening. "Go ahead and give Mr. Gupta access to whatever his team needs."

"Yes, ma'am." James answered.

"But don't leave them alone. Assign someone to watch over them." She smirked at Akash.

Akash stood there and rolled his eyes.

"You can go back to your office now," Reena snapped. "I'll let your team see whatever they want."

"How long have you been without a chef?" Akash dropped the question like a demand.

"I'm working on it. Properly trained, competent chefs are hard to find." Reena answered stoically.

"You probably won't get anyone like Sonny."

Reena flinched at the mention of her brother. She missed him. "That does not mean I can't try."

"A chef would be bring people in."

"I am aware of that, Mr. Fifty-one Percent. I am simply not willing to compromise on quality." She narrowed her eyes at him and leaned back in her chair. "I also need front desk staff, housekeeping, and janitorial staff. Not to mention spa staff."

Akash shrugged. "Close the spa. Operating it is expensive if you don't have the staff to support it."

Reena stared at him. He was right. She had told her father as much; he hadn't listened.

"I could have a nail esthetician come in once or twice a week and handle mani and pedi appointments. The rest of the spa can be closed while we work on other things." Reena mused out loud. She focused on Akash. "The reality is, your people can look at our books all day, but I have already done that. My problem is that the hotel is outdated in terms of decor and ambiance. We need a new look, but more than that, we need staff. I have an intern working on that right now."

"Excuse me, Ms. Pandya," James said. "The intern is here."

"Send her in." She looked at Akash. "You can meet that intern that I had—" She stopped herself. "The intern who is going to help with my staffing issues." Reena stood as a petite young woman with dark curly hair and energetic dark eyes entered her office.

"Kirti Doshi, this is Akash Gupta. Mr. Gupta, my intern, Ms. Doshi."

If Akash had been irritated before, it was nothing to how he looked now, jaw clenched, eyes blazing, vein ticking at his temple. Reena turned to Kirti. The young woman's brown skin had an angry flush to it, her mouth was crushed shut as she stared at Akash.

"Reena," Akash said between clenched teeth. "You must be kidding. *This* is your intern?" His growl was laced with irritation that matched Kirti's anger. *"This* is the person you've been going on about?"

"Yes. What of it?" Reena snapped at him. Now he was going to question her choice of *intern*?

"She's my sister."

Chapter Four

How had he not known that Reena's intern was his stepsister? He racked his brain. Reena never mentioned her name.

Kirti stared him down. Their dislike for one another was mutual.

Reena looked from one to the other. "I'm so confused."

"I am his *stepsister,* unfortunately for me," Kirti retorted. "We have the same mother."

Reena raised an eyebrow at him. The accusation on her face was clear. In all the time they'd been together, he'd never mentioned Kirti to her, not that it mattered now.

Akash exhaled and turned away from both of them. This was too much. There wasn't enough coffee or chai for this. Was it too early for whiskey?

"His mom married my dad, when I was like two," Kirti clarified. She turned to Reena. "In any case, I have an update for you."

Reena smiled at the young woman. She was intelligent, resourceful, enthusiastic and full of energy.

"Tell me." Reena motioned to the chair opposite her desk.

Kirti did not sit, instead, she walked around to her side of the desk. "Let me show you." She poised her hands over Reena's keyboard. "May I?"

Reena nodded. "Of course."

Kirti hesitated. "Um, is it okay he's here?"

"Well, he has fifty-one percent of my hotel, so yes," Reena stated, throwing him a glare.

"At fifty-one percent, it's technically my hotel." The words fell out of his mouth as a reflex, before he had a chance to think about them. A flicker of pain went through Reena's eyes, which he felt in his chest, but it was gone as fast as it came.

Whatever. She had been ready to hurt one of the two people he cared about most in the world. He should have known that a relationship with Reena would never work. Aside from his two sisters, every relationship he'd ever had had fallen apart.

That included Kirti and his mom.

Kirti was typing away at Reena's computer, talking the whole time. "The idea we had was to hire single moms and train them in various aspects of the hotel industry, and make a day care in the employee wing, which goes unused—except for your room, and mine, now."

"Right." Reena flicked a glance at him.

He remembered Reena telling him about this concept. She had been so excited, so full of hope. He had been excited for her. They had spent the whole evening talking about the best strategy for training various personnel. Until they got bored with that and had moved on to other things. He cleared his throat as if that would clear the memory from his brain.

"So, now." Kirti dramatically hit a button and stepped back. "We are good to go."

Akash walked around to the other side of the desk and stood behind Reena. He could tell she'd washed her hair today, because the delicate scent of flowers surrounded her.

It was driving him mad, but he gritted his teeth and leaned over to look at the plans.

Kirti had pulled up an impressive spreadsheet that detailed a work and day care schedule, and how long each position would require for training.

Reena shook her head and smiled at Kirti. "This is amazing. Yes. Get started. You have applicants ready to go?"

"Yes. My mom," she glanced quickly at Akash, "is a social worker. She meets women who need work every day. I have at least ten candidates who have been through the interview and vetting processes, and ready to go. When they are not being trained, they will run the day care."

"Pay them," Reena said.

"What?" Kirti asked.

"We just received a chunk of money from Gupta

Equity, might as well use it for good—pay them when they run the day care."

"I have to approve that," Akash interrupted.

Both women turned to him, their jaws set, daring him.

He cleared his throat again. "Approved."

Kirti grinned. "That will help immensely! And you have to check out what my team and I did with those rooms in the employee wing."

"I'll be sure to stop by," Reena said.

"Me, too," Akash added, clearing his throat again.

The women glanced at him as if they had forgotten he was there.

"Maybe check out why your throat is so phlegmy," Reena said.

"How much does Kirti get?" He asked, ignoring Reena's sass.

"This is an unpaid internship. I have one semester of college left. I get a couple credits." Kirti was curt, until she turned her attention to Reena. "I just wanted to learn from Reena. She's a successful, local South Asian businessperson."

She nodded at Reena and shot Akash a glare before leaving the office.

Reena went back to her computer, as if Akash weren't even there. He started to leave.

"You never even mentioned her—not once in six months." Reena spoke to him, her eyes still on the computer. "It's clear she's not much fonder of you than you are of her." Reena shrugged. "She's spunky and she has good ideas. Besides she's working for free."

She smirked at him. "It's actually to both our benefits to let her work here."

"We need an event." He spoke decisively, as though he hadn't heard the betrayal, the hurt in her voice. But he had. He just didn't know how to respond—and so it was easier to ignore it.

"Excuse me?" She stopped typing and looked at him.

"We need an event for the hotel. To make it profitable, faster. We need to become the place that companies hold their retreats—"

"I have the Patel/Shah wedding six weeks from now, early October. Then about a month later, I have the Shah/Jones wedding."

He opended his mouth to comment.

"No relation. You know Shah is a common name." She paused, her lips pursed in an expression that Akash recognized as her contemplative look. "But yes, company retreats would be a regular thing that would mean guaranteed income." She hesitated. "Do you have any contacts for that sort of thing? Maybe you could explore it."

"I'll check the companies in the area. See who does retreats," Akash offered, making notes on his phone.

"Sure," Reena replied, nodding. She went back to her computer.

Akash watched her for a minute before leaving. He was still angry at her, but his heart filled with pride, watching her in her element. He had never considered her incompetent – not for a second. In fact her quick instincts and large dose of courage were some of things he'd most admired about her.

He hadn't told her about Kirti because he tried to forget Kirti existed. Much like he tried to deny his mother's existence. He turned and headed out. Kirti was in the outer office, chatting with James. Akash met her gaze briefly before nodding at the both of them and leaving.

He made it to the elevator before the memories assaulted him.

He was eight. Asha was six and Nila must have been four. His mother had made their lunches before they left school that day. She looked tired and sad. He had heard loud voices coming from his parents' bedroom the night before. He thought he'd heard his mother crying.

But he had heard it before. And whenever it happened earlier, his mother was always happier by the time they came home from school.

She had insisted on driving them to school that day, as opposed to the driver their father had hired.

"I can drive my own children to school, Pradeep," his mother had snapped.

She piled them into the car, and they played word games on the way to school. Nila had been dropped off at her pre-school first,then he and Asha at the elementary school. His mother stopped him as he got out of the car, her face sad. "I love you, Akash. Take care of your sisters, huh? Like a good boy."

Akash hugged his mother, a small knot in the pit of his stomach. Even at eight, he knew something was off.

And he was correct. When he got home, he went right to the kitchen, where his mother had always had a snack waiting for them. But she wasn't there. Only Margie, their nanny/cook was.

"Where's Mom?" Asha asked.

Margie avoided their eyes.

Akash had demanded an answer. "Where is she? Where is our mom?"

Still, Margie did not answer.

Akash went to their parents' room. He was light-headed. Asha followed him. "Bhaiya. Where are her clothes?" Their mother's side of the closet was nearly empty.

Akash took his sister's hand and pulled her out of the room, shutting the door behind them. They were too little to have their own phones so he couldn't call his mom or his dad. But he knew.

He went back to Margie. The ground underneath him gave way, and he was sick to his stomach. "She left us, didn't she? Our Mom. She left us."

Margie's eyes filled with tears, but she hadn't responded.

Asha started crying. Nila was tugging at him; she was hungry. He wanted to scream, and cry and run and go find her, but he was powerless. Dad would be home soon, but right now, they were alone. Besides, he had to take care of his sisters.

He lifted Nila to the breakfast bar and put her plate in front of her. He held Asha tight.

"It's okay, Asha."

"I want Mommy!" She wailed. "I want Mommy! I want Mommy!"

He wanted Mommy, too. He wanted to cry and scream, but his sisters needed him. They were littler than him. He held Asha and eventually distracted her with her favorite TV show. Their Mother had taken her clothes and gone away, and he had no way to find her.

As if the universe had nothing else to do than force him to confront his family members today, his mother was waiting for him in the reception area of his office.

"Why are you here?" he kept his voice even, devoid of emotion. Anger and betrayal swirled inside him at the sight of her, but he refused to acknowledge that anger in any way.

"Akash." His mother's voice was soft, concerned. Jaymini Doshi was tall and fit, and though she was just over fifty, she could easily have been mistaken for Asha's older sister. Her long hair was wrapped in a small bun, her make up was minimal. She was dressed in dark jeans and a silk blouse.

He simply nodded that he heard her, not turning to face her. "Are you okay?"

"Why the sudden interest?"

"It's not sudden." She sighed. "Kirti texted. Told me you are both working at Lulu's."

"I own it now." He turned to her. "You came into town all the way from the burbs because Kirti and I are working in the same office?"

"I'm…well I'm staying with Asha. In town." She paused. "Are you alright? You seem…not yourself."

"How would you know if I was myself or not?" Akash responded curtly, without even turning to her.

"I can see it. And not because I'm your mother. But because it's there. For everyone to see. As your mother, I am the only one brave enough to confront you with it."

"You shouldn't be so brave." He swept past her to his office door.

"Akash. Something has happened to you. I can see it." She insisted.

"I'm fine. You can go. It's what you're good at." He had felt the ground disintegrate beneath his feet when his mother had left. He hadn't felt grounded again until he met Reena. That was gone now, too.

His father had returned very late that night. The three of them were piled together on Akash's bed. Asha and Nila had cried themselves to sleep, while Akash held their hands. His father had peeked into his room and found him awake.

"Akash." His father's voice had sounded sad, defeated.

"Dad. When is Mom coming home?" He bit his lower lip to keep it from trembling.

He shook his head. "She is not coming home."

His words punched a hole in Akash's belly. He ruffled Akash's hair and left the room. In the darkness, alone with his sleeping sisters, Akash finally let his tears fall. His mom was gone.

She wasn't there when he woke in the morning, but Margie was. She got them up and ready for school, made their lunches. But she didn't know what they liked. Akash couldn't believe they had to do something as banal as go to school when their mother had left them. The girls cried, asking for their mother.

"Where is my dad?" He had asked, though he knew the answer.

"He went to work," was the reply.

When they came home, however, their mother was there. Akash's heart leaped. Their mother had come home. Dad had been wrong, and everything was going to be okay. The girls ran to her, giving hugs and kisses, but Akash held back.

"Hi, beta," she had said, enveloping him in a hug. He hugged her back.

"I knew Dad was wrong. I knew you would come back." He squeezed her tight. "I just knew it."

"Akash. I found an apartment just a couple blocks from here. Dad and I are not going to live together anymore."

Akash stiffened in her arms. He pulled away from her, his heart breaking.

"What about us?" asked Asha.

"Well, you all can live here and live with me." His mother had smiled like this was the best idea ever. "You'll have two houses."

The girls were skeptical but wanted to believe, so they did. Akash knew the truth. His mother was leaving him. He did not know why; he only knew that she was leaving him and things would never be the same.

* * *

After that, things moved quickly. His mother officially moved out but saw them every day after school. Akash clung to his father, distancing himself from the mother he no longer trusted. His father didn't smile as much anymore, and Akash had heard him on the phone.

"I took care of her. I provided everything. She could have gone to school or done whatever she wanted," his father bemoaned. "How can she be happy without me, when I am miserable without her?"

His mother tried reaching Akash, but he had blocked her out. He identified with the brokenhearted father he saw every day. Not the smiling, lighthearted woman his mother was transforming into. He hadn't even really cared when she remarried. The three of them had met Rakesh Uncle, and he seemed nice enough. He had a daughter, Kirti, who was a year or so younger than Nila. His sisters took to her immediately, reveling in a baby sister. But what little Akash saw was a small girl who had stolen his mother's attention, who got to live with her all the time.

That was the last straw. As far as he was concerned, his mother no longer cared for him. He never understood why his sisters insisted on going to see her. He and his father would do things together when the girls were with their mother. Asha asked him every time to come, telling him all the fun things that they would do. Akash didn't want to leave his father all alone, he felt sad that his father seemed to have no one but him.

He was also very angry with his mother, so he never went. The more time that passed in this manner, the more it stayed the same.

"Akash. I can see you are hurting. Even if no one else can. Something has happened." His mother insisted.

"You know what? You don't know anything, don't come around being a mother all of a sudden to me—"

"All of a sudden? I have been here, twenty minutes away for your whole life. I left your father. Not you. Your sisters have understood that. Why haven't you?"

"Because I was old enough to know better. Because I heard him talking to Kaka." The pain of overhearing that conversation still had a sting. "About how he …missed you. About how he worked hard to give you everything," he furrowed his brow, "and you left anyway." Akash was drained. Between interacting with Reena today, running into Kirti and now his mother, emotions he thought he had settled long ago returned with a vengeance.

"Old enough? You were eight." She picked up her bag from the lounge chair in the waiting area and made for the door. "Did he tell you why I left?" His mother rested sad eyes on him. "Did you ever even bother to ask?"

Akash had not. He simply stared at her.

"I didn't think so." She walked toward the door and opened it. "Making assumptions about people is a typical male Gupta trait. Congrats. You're just like your father." She walked through door and left.

Again.

Chapter Five

It had been almost seven weeks. Reena needed her stuff. She had almost been living at Akash's place. She had purchased a few necessities—shampoo, a new toothbrush, some new makeup—in an effort to avoid going to his apartment, but she could not avoid it much longer. Her favorite suits were there, and her present budget did not allow for simply repurchasing them. James was already commenting on the fact that she had worn the lime-colored suit twice this week.

"I thought you were helping Kirti get this program on the road," she said to her assistant.

"That girl does not need help. She has already lined up four families and they are currently cleaning the employee wing. We start official training next week."

Reena was impressed. "Start two on front desk and two on scheduling. Anybody know how to cook?"

"No love there. Sorry." He eyed her. "But we have Anu Patel and her mother stopping by to take a look at the place. Again." He rolled his eyes. "Planner is bringing them. But do not wear that lime thing again. Where is that gorgeous cream suit? Or the lavender one?"

"Dry cleaning." She lied. They were at Akash's. She would have to go and get them. "I'll stop off tonight after work."

"I can go for you now," James offered.

"No." She snapped at the poor man.

"Okay." James backed off, eyeing her. "No need to snap."

"Why is she being rude now, James?" Akash walked in as if he belonged there. He'd been there every day and showed no sign of not showing up. If they'd still been together, Reena might have been thrilled. They were decidedly not together, so it was ludicrous that her heart did a happy flip every time he showed up to work. *He didn't want her. And she didn't want him.*

"She wants to pick up her own dry cleaning. Which is odd. She never did before."

"James." Reena did not look up from her computer, aware of the flush on her face.

James looked from his boss to Akash and then back at Reena. His eyes widened, and he opened his mouth as if to say something. But instead, he held up his hands in surrender. "Fine, I'll stop. In any case, you need to get your suits."

"What's wrong with the one she has on?" Akash

raked his gaze over her as she looked up and she heated even more. Damn it.

"She's worn it twice. This week. Plus, we have a wealthy Indian family coming tomorrow to check in about their wedding, and we can't have our leader in yesterday's clothes." James explained.

"James. Your desk awaits you." She grinned at him. "And please close the door."

She looked at Akash and shrugged as James left. "It's the Patel wedding in October. The mom is a bit... much. Needs to check in regularly."

"Sounds great." Akash nodded. "I'm looking into a retreat. I believe Joshi Family Law might be looking to start a yearly retreat."

"JFL? Really?" Reena was impressed in spite of herself. "Amar Virani's sister works there. She married into the family. I could put in a call."

She started to make a note.

"That's not necessary. I can handle it on my own." Akash was curt.

She pressed her mouth tight and shrugged. "Up to you." She deleted the note. For one split second, they had felt like a team. "I'll need to stop by tonight for my things."

"You can't."

"What do you mean I can't? I need my clothes. I don't have money for a whole new wardrobe right now." Reena whisper-shouted.

"I'm staying at Asha's right now. The place is being...fumigated. Your stuff is probably there. I had to move things in a hurry. I'll get it and bring it to your place," Akash said, not meeting her eyes.

"Fine. I need all my clothes."

"I can bring it all over tonight."

She sighed. The last thing she needed was to be alone with Akash Gupta in her hotel room.

Akash glanced at his phone once more. Five minutes since he'd last checked. It was close to ten p.m. and Reena had not yet texted that she was home so he could drop off her stuff. The truth was he had sold the condo and moved into a smaller apartment some blocks away. Her stuff had already been packed into a few suitcases. He could have returned it weeks ago. In fact, he should have. He had simply never had the time.

Or so he told himself.

He stood to stretch and glanced out the window of his new home. Gone were the floor-to-ceiling windows of that condo. Gone also was the view of the water and the city lights. That was really all he missed.

He and Reena had stood in front of his window in each other's arms, time and time again. They had made love in the dark to the light of only the city more times than he could count. The lights reflected in her hazel eyes and dancing off her naked body had only added to her natural beauty. In those moments, they were the only two people on earth. In those moments, he was lost in her, and there had been nowhere else he'd rather be, no one else he'd rather have been with. His heart ached not being with her.

The new place was significantly smaller, just off the

water. No floor-to-ceiling windows here, but the view from his balcony of the city and the harbor in the distance was beautiful. He had opted for a one bedroom, one bath that had a reasonable kitchen so he could still cook. Whatever hadn't fit, he had put in storage. He turned from the window. This apartment had no memories of Reena associated with it, yet she was everywhere, emerging from the shadows of his mind.

His phone buzzed. Reena. I'm home. He grabbed the suitcases and drove over to Lulu's. He parked in the back where the employees parked and made his way to her small suite.

She opened the door, already in her sweats, her hair tied up in a messy bun. Dark circles were mildly visible under her eyes, but that was the only sign of her stress. Other than that, she looked like the powerhouse she was. So clearly, *she* put the power in her power suits.

"Hey," he said as she stepped aside to let him in.

"Hey." She did not make eye contact.

Walking past her was a unique form of torture. She had most certainly showered upon coming home and she smelled like her lemon ginger body wash and that scent that was uniquely Reena. It hit him in his core. His body immediately responded to her like a Pavlovian dog. He quickly brushed past her into the suite to set down the suitcases.

The whole place smelled like fresh lemon, with a hint of ginger and…it must be cardamom from chai she reheated. It was the scent of comfort that he had allowed himself to get used to. He was torn between wanting to scoop her up in his arms and the hurt and anger simmering inside him.

"Thank you," she said. She hadn't moved from her spot.

"You want to make sure you got everything? I had packed in a rush—things were unorganized." He stepped back from her and the bags.

She sighed. "Sure." She opened the bags. "I'll just put it all away and that way I'll know. You can have a seat, if you want." She nodded to the small sofa and plush chair in the "living area" of the suite.

"Sure." He sat down. His apartment was slightly larger than this suite. She had a kitchenette, of which he knew she used only the microwave.

Reena bustled around as she emptied the suitcases. Each item she removed held a memory. He silently winced, as if he were in physical pain.

He'd get over it. It was better this way.

She did not look at him, even when she brushed past him to the bathroom to put away her makeup. True to her word, twenty minutes later, she was unpacked. She faced him. "It's all here."

It took Akash a moment to get his body to stand. No matter what was going on between them, no matter what sort of anger still lingered, he did not want to leave her presence.

Damn it. He missed her.

His brain finally took over his heart. He stood and held his breath as he walked past her. She opened the door and he walked out of her life without another word.

Chapter Six

To her great satisfaction, Reena was able to wait until Akash finally walked out of her suite and the door was shut before her tears fell. Being in the same space with Akash—being close enough to catch his scent, to feel heat from his body or even just hear his voice—it was too intense. It was too much to share intimate space knowing he was no longer hers.

Her heart cracked the minute she had opened the door to him. Thick dark hair, disheveled, and simmering dark eyes, weary. She'd actually been home for hours, and had put off texting him as long as she could, but she needed her clothes.

She closed the door behind him, his scent lingered, her suite all the more empty for having had him there to begin with.

She made her way to the sitting area and slid into the chair he had just occupied. It was still warm from his body. The pain of him brushing roughly past her, dismissed as if she were a stranger on the subway, was all consuming. She was unable to keep the tears from falling. His scent, his heat, everything about him that she had come to associate with comfort was lost to her now. She sobbed alone, curled up in the chair he had just vacated, until she had nothing left.

"You smell amazing."Akash reached an arm around and pulled her close. He had been home for a while and was already changed into sweats and T-shirt. She was lying next to him on his gargantuan bed, still in work clothes. He smelled amazing too, like spices, since he had been cooking.

"That is a weird thing to say," she teased and pulled back slightly."Are you sniffing me?"

"I am," he said unabashed. His lips grazed her neck as he pulled her even closer, encompassing her in his embrace. His other hand was in her hair. Locked in Akash's embrace, Reena was safe, cherished, loved in a way she had never experienced before. She was visited by the knowledge that she could tell him anything and he would love her regardless. She could even fail at something, and he would love her, stand by her, be there for her.

"I love everything about you," he murmured in between kisses that moved from her neck southward. "Your hair, your skin, your scent. My favorite thing about you, however, is your brain. Your out-of-the-box

*thinking is probably the biggest turn-on ever." He was
unbuttoning her suit and the blouse beneath it.*

*"My brain?" She had chuckled. "That's what you
love best?"*

*He glanced up at her and nodded. "Uh-huh." He
returned to kissing her.*

*"You know what I love best about you?" She had
feathered her fingers into his hair, and he glanced up
at her from her belly.*

*She'd had something snarky to say, but just then,
the look in his eyes was more than desire—it was love.
His love was unconditional, the rarest of birds.*

*"Everything," she had whispered. "I love every-
thing about you best."*

Reena was pulled from her reverie by the buzzing
of her phone. *Sonny.* Finally, her brother returned her
messages. She tapped to answer.

"Hey."

"Hey."

She hated being awkward with Sonny. But she had
manipulated him into doing things that had only served
Lulu's. Not to mention the whole Rahul debacle.

Reena had been the one who had erased the video
that proved that Rahul had cheated, leaving her brother
without proof when he confronted Asha. Not her fin-
est moment, but she still wished that he wasn't mad at
her. He didn't know about Akash, of course. No one
did. There had been an almost unspoken agreement between them not to tell their families, just yet. Neither
of them had ever prioritized a relationship before, so

they were still feeling it out to some degree. Though there had been more recent moments when each of them had expressed possibly telling a sibling.

Reena almost wished they had. She could use her big brother right now.

"You haven't been to Sunday dinner in awhile," he said.

"I've been—"

"You're not busy. You're avoiding me."

True. She remained silent.

"What? Have I silenced Reena Pandya?" Sonny joked. She heard the smile in his voice and relaxed.

"I'm giving you a chance to be Mom and Dad's favorite for a few weeks," she teased. They both knew that their youngest brother, Jai, was the favorite.

"Have you been making your own chai?" he asked.

"I have tried." And failed.

"Stop drinking your own chai. Come down tomorrow morning and get real chai from someone who knows how to make it."

Reena's eye filled with tears. She had missed her brother. She nodded into the phone so he wouldn't hear her tears.

"Reena?"

She swallowed her tears. "I'll see you in the morning." Her voice was thick with tears and though they both knew it, they both chose to ignored it.

"I wanted to give you a heads-up that Mom might be calling you," her big brother told her.

Her tears instantly dried as she went on high alert. "You could have started with that."

"It's fine.They are getting ready to go on some world tour vacation."

"They are?"

"That's why she's going to call you."

She wanted to make sure that Reena knew what she was doing while they were away. Forget that Reena had been learning everything about Lulu's since she was ten. Other children played games; Reena played hotelier.

Reena had always been taken in by the fact that her parents had built this from the ground up. That before they came, this building was nothing. She wanted to do right by Lulu's. She wanted to do right by her parents.

But at this point, she was failing everyone.

Chapter Seven

Akash went to the office the next morning to take care of business for his own company, AG, before heading over to Lulu's. He was on the phone with an investor, when his father popped into his office. "How's the hotel?"

Akash spoke into his phone. "I'll have to get back to you on that later, Jorge. Thanks."

He turned his attention to his father. "The hotel is struggling, but it'll be fine. We have a few things to work on. Same inefficiencies that we usually see." He shrugged. He loved his father, but in business, he was somewhat of a shark.

Which was why Akash did not want his father involved with Lulu's, in any way. Reena had assumed that Gupta Equity was involved, and Akash had every intention of letting her continue to believe that.

His intentions when he had decided to give money to Lulu's were much different than what was currently playing out. But the situation had been different when he had first approached Reena's father with his idea. Things changed, he was simply making the best of it.

Sometimes, things don't work the way you'd expect.

"I'm thinking to go sailing this weekend, want to join?" his father asked. Akash had learned to sail from his father; they kept that boat docked in Annapolis. But he knew his father was asking as a formality, he wanted to take a woman. After the divorce, his father had never remarried, but he was never really alone, either. Pradeep Gupta was a handsome man, he took care of himself and he enjoyed dating.

Akash had asked his father about this some years ago.

"How come you never remarried, Dad? Mom did."

His father had shrugged. "I married your mom because she was the love of my life. Losing your mom was the most painful thing I have ever gone through. I have no desire to go down that road again, so I keep it light." He had looked Akash in the eye in a rare moment of singular attention. "Keep that in mind."

"Nah. You go ahead." Akash smiled at his father. "I know you want to take Namrata Auntie." She was his latest fling.

"I'll cancel if you say yes."

Akash laughed and put his hands up. "No. I'm good. You go ahead."

His father shrugged and started to leave.

"Hey, Dad." His father turned back. He should just

ask him why his mom left. It was a simple question. The words were stuck in his throat. "Have fun."

"Will do." His father came back into his office, concern on his face. "You okay, Beta? You seem…off."

Akash made a show of frowning and shaking his head. His heart was broken. The one woman he had ever loved was gone; he had broken up with her and now he was barley keeping his head over the waters of despair. "I'm fine. Just a lot to do with that hotel."

His father nodded, dubious. "If you say so. How's your sister holding up?"

"She's a trooper." Akash filled with pride. "Hanging out with Mom, I think. She'll be all right."

"I'll stop by tonight. Check on her," his father said as he left.

"She'll be happy to see you," Akash answered. Asha and her wedding planner had gotten most of their wedding money back—certainly, Lulu's had returned everything. They were having an issue with Ginger and Cardamom, the caterer, but Akash knew Asha would be able to handle it.

"I haven't forgotten—your big birthday is coming up, and that's when I'll make good on my promise to make you partner."

Akash forced a smile. "Sure of course."

His father left. Akash had no intention whatsoever of becoming a partner at Gupta Equity. He just hadn't told his father that.

Chapter Eight

Reena met Toral Patel and her daughter Anu, along with their planner, Lalita, in the main lobby of Lulu's.

"Good to see you, Lalita." Reena said.

"You as well. You remember Toral Patel and her daughter Anu."

"Of course." Reena smiled at the women. "The big day is only five weeks away. It will be here before we know it. How can I help you today?"

"Well," Mrs. Patel started. "I am concerned that you do not have a chef."

Lalita shot Reena an *I'm sorry* look. "Mrs. Patel was asking about the cuisine in the hotel."

Reena did not miss a beat. "Of course. As you know, we have already contracted the company Ginger and Cardamom as well as The Masala Hut for catering of your events. And for desserts, we have For Goodness' Cakes. We have worked closely with them in the past and they are one hundred percent reliable and delicious. You may recall the fantastic crepes you sampled with Lalita." Reena flashed her conspiratorial smile, instantly reminding herself of Akash. "That being said, we are also very close to hiring a new chef. We're very particular here at Lulu's, so we can't just bring anyone on to our staff." Reena smiled.

She said the right thing, because Mrs. Patel smiled, knowingly. "Of course. But once you have the right chef, I would love to do a tasting."

"Of course. Lalita can arrange all of that." Reena glanced at Lalita who looked relieved. "But as we are close, we would need to keep the main items with the current caterers."

"Would you like another tour?" Reena asked. She noticed a few new faces at the front desk.

"That won't be necessary, Ms. Pandya." Anu spoke up, quite the rare occurrence when her mother was around. "We've seen the area many times and attended many events here."

"Perfect. Final payment is not due for another couple weeks, so we are all set with that. I'll be sure to let Lalita know when we hire a chef, and she can let you know," Reena said. She nodded at Lalita, who smiled and nodded back.

"I would prefer for you to let us know directly, when you hire a chef," Mrs. Patel demanded.

"Of course." Reena sighed and fixed her gaze on the

woman. "I will be happy to let you and Lalita know when we have completed our search."

Lalita was a good wedding coordinator, but having worked with her in the past, Reena knew all too well that the woman did not handle demanding clients all too well. And that could make a demanding client *her* problem. Which was why she really wished someone like Sangeeta Parikh was the planner on this affair.

Sangeeta was a wedding planner who had only recently gone out on her own. They had worked together on Asha Gupta's wedding, and Reena had found her more than competent and likeable. Sangeeta was probably as close to a friend as Reena had.

Reena excused herself and went to the front desk. The two new trainees were listening to Janki, the manager, intently. One of them seemed to be easily following instruction on the use of their software. The other seemed to be struggling.

"Hello." Reena interrupted them. "I wanted to introduce myself. I am Reena Pandya."

Their eyes lit up. "The big boss," said the one who had ease on the computer. "I'm Sabina."

"And I'm Ishani." The other woman smiled but kept her attention on the computer.

"It's nice to meet you both." Reena smiled. "I'm very happy to have you on board. We really need the help."

"Of course," said Sabina. "We're happy to be here."

"Yes," agreed Ishani, though she was still clearly frazzled.

Reena nodded at Janki. "Let's get them to proficiency, shall we?"

"Of course, Ms. Pandya," Janki answered.

"I'll leave you in capable hands." Reena smiled at the two women.

Reena turned to make her way up to her office. Her father still had his office for another few weeks, then, according to her mother, who had in fact called after she had hung up with Sonny, her parents were taking a well-deserved and very overdue extended vacation.

Her mother had not simply called to tell her about their vacation, she was not-so-subtly making sure that Reena was prepared to handle things while they were gone.

"Mom. It'll be fine. I've been doing this my whole life."

"Yes. But never alone."

"You were actually supposed to hand over control of Lulu's to me this year anyway. That was the agreement, it just got....derailed."

"Your father made that agreement with you. I was... skeptical." Her mother said with absolutely no emotion.

A rock landed in Reena stomach. "What do you mean...skeptical? You're the one who taught me."

"You simply have much more to learn, which was evidenced by the whole Asha/Rahul debacle. You should have known your brother was of the conscience to spill the beans, and averted that."

Reena's anger had made her speechless. Her mother had always had high expectations of her, but Reena had always thought that was designed so that Reena

*would always surpass those expectations. Which she
regularly did.*

"Mom. What are you—"

*"It's no matter now. You're father wants this trip, so
we will go. You'll simply have to do your best."* With
that her mother had hung up.

She popped her head into her father's office and was
surprised to see Akash in there. He was leaning over
her father's computer, pointing to something on the
screen. Today's suit was gray, and he had opted out of
the tie. The suit material stretched over his muscles as
he reached over to point something out to her father.
He was irritatingly handsome.

"What's going on here?" She barged in, immediately on alert for further business dealings going on
behind her back.

"Oh. Reena, beti. Come in." Her father beckoned.
"Akash here was telling me about getting JFL to hold
their retreat here."

"Yes, he had mentioned it." She tried not to look at
him as he straightened and stepped back from the computer. He put his hands in his pockets, throwing the
jacket back and revealing the formfitting crisp white
shirt.

"Don't you have a contact there? He doesn't seem
to be making headway." Her father interrupted her
gawking.

"Really?" Reena smirked, turning to Akash. "As
previously mentioned to you, I do have a contact

through one of our caterers. I'm happy to reach out to him." She paused. "With your permission of course."

Akash's jaw ticked and annoyance took over his dark eyes.

Reena grinned more broadly, the picture of innocence.

"Of course," he said. "Please do reach out, Ms. Pandya."

Chapter Nine

Reena mock saluted him, then turned and left the office. She was even more attractive when she was annoying him. The lavender suit was beautiful on her. He hadn't cared for it when she had first brought it to his place, but he had completely had a change of thought when she'd worn it to work the next day. The suit was tailored to just graze her curves but remained professional.

What he had truly enjoyed about the suit was slowly removing it from her body just a few weeks ago, leaving only the diamond studs he'd given her.

She didn't have them on today.

He followed her out of her father's office; he couldn't help himself.

"You're welcome," she said without turning around.

"For what?"

"For saving you," she added as she stopped at her assistant's desk. "James, send Amar Virani and Divya Shah emails confirming that we have them for the Patel Wedding. And would Amar be able to get me in touch with his sister Anita at JFL? And cc Mr. Gupta on that email." She nodded at James as she hustled into her office.

"Thank you," he said. "Speaking of Amar Virani, there isn't a charge for Ginger and Cardamom, for day-of catering for Asha's wedding."

Something flashed in her hazel eyes, but Akash could not tell what.

"You'll have to take that up with the wedding planner, Sangeeta. As far as my notes go, everything paid to Lulu's was returned." Reena's voice had a definite edge that he had not heard before.

"I'll look into it," he said.

Reena paused and turned her head to the side before going behind her desk to face him. She reached into a drawer and pulled out a small velvet box and held it out to him. It was a punch in the gut. He backed away from the box. "Those are yours. A gift."

She looked at him, her face a mask to her emotions. "A very expensive gift that I no longer enjoy." She met his eyes, and he knew they were both thinking of the moment he had given them to her. Their six-month anniversary. "Put the box in your pocket, Akash. Don't make this messy. We are working together, after all."

"Anything for the hotel." He answered as amiably as he could. He reached for the small box as if it might bite him. It felt foreign in his hands, but then he hadn't held onto the box for very long.

"My sentiments, exactly." Reena smiled sweetly, clearly trying to annoy him. It was working.

"What happened with the Patel wedding?"

"We're still on. Got to love a big fat Indian wedding." She grinned.

"Sounds like you have it under control."

"Of course I do." She sighed. "What I really need is an on-site chef. I'm interviewing a few next week. If they seem capable, I'll have to set up their tasting interviews."

"Have James send Gemma the details," Akash said.

"I can interview a chef on my own." She shuffled papers on her desk.

He stared at her. She was right. She absolutely could. "I have no doubt. I still want to be there." Apparently, he enjoyed torturing himself. "There will be food."

She rolled her eyes. "James." She called out.

Her assistant appeared at the door. "I heard, Ms. Pandya."

She shook her head at him. "Thank you. And please close the door."

James closed the door with a satisfying click.

"I was just leaving anyway." Akash walked to the door.

"What is the deal between you and Kirti?" Reena asked before he reached it.

He turned around to face her. "That is personal, and we no longer have that kind of relationship."

"You never shared this with me when we were together anyway. But I need to know now, because you are both on my team, so-to-speak." She kept her tone businesslike, while wearing no smile at all. "I need to know that we can all work together effectively."

Akash sighed, his hand still on the knob. He really did not want to get into this, but Reena had a point. If they were all going be working together, it might be better to get things out in the open. Just the basics, at least.

He walked back in and took a seat on her sofa. He looked out the window behind Reena's desk. "You know my mom left when we were little. My dad got custody of us. I went to see my mom the first few times, but I always felt bad, leaving my dad all alone. He always looked so…" He felt lost in memory for a moment as images of his father, sad and angry when they would go see their mother, flooded his mind. "Besides, she never even really fought for us. She didn't want us. She didn't want me, at least."

Reena's expression softened, and for a moment, he longed to seek comfort in her arms. In the solace he knew he'd find in her kiss. In her body.

But just as quickly as the craving for her overwhelmed him, he tamped it down. He didn't need or want her pity.

Akash remembered sitting in his mother's new apartment after the divorce while she oiled Asha's hair and played with Nila. Akash had wanted answers, but every time he had asked her why she left, she avoided the subject. She would just say that things were better this way. That he would understand when he was older, and in a relationship of his own.

Young Akash could not understand how things were better if they weren't all together. Especially when his father looked miserable every time they left to spend time with their mother. Shaking his head, he brought himself back to the present.

"Then she met Rakesh Uncle. He had a daughter, two years old. Kirti." He chuckled in spite of himself. "That spunk you love, she must have been born with it. Mom—Jaymini—had her hands full." He shrugged, avoiding Reena's eyes. "Jaymini's time was taken up mothering Kirti. Asha and Nila loved her, but I just felt left out. Like I didn't belong.

"So, I guess eventually I dismissed them both from my life. As she got older, Kirti and I had to interact for birthdays, Diwali, etc., but we never really got along." He shrugged. "Though, if I'm honest, that was mostly on me." He'd never even admitted that to himself before, and here he was, admitting it to Reena. That was the power she had over him. They weren't even together, and he still wanted to be a better man for her.

Reena held him in her gaze. "So, you're close to Asha and Nila, but not Kirti."

"I had my sisters during the week. I took care of them while my dad worked late—which was quite often. I helped with homework, boy drama and girl drama—hey, don't look so surprised! I'm a good listener."

At this she nodded, a smile on her face. "Agreed."

"I was the first person Nila came out to, even before

Asha. She said she picked me to be first because she knew I would love her no matter what." He dropped his voice. "She was right. They were everything to me. Still are. Asha and Nila are the only people I can count on." He froze his gaze on Reena for a moment. "My mom and Kirti have each other."

"That was a long time ago, though, wasn't it?" Reena leaned toward him, still behind her desk, her voice soft.

"So?"

"You're all adults now." She shrugged, but her tone was kind. "Yes, we have baggage, but maybe it's time to let the past be. Maybe it's time to grow up and move on."

Leave it to Reena to lay it out in black and white.

"It's not that easy," he mumbled. "You should know. Are you and Sonny still not talking?"

Her eyes lit up. "He called the other night. It's a step."

"Glad to hear it." And he really was. Reena wasn't close to many people. Not speaking with Sonny would certainly have taken a toll on her. "I know how much he means to you."

She gave him that small smile that he knew she reserved only for him. Damn, he missed her smiles.

"You have a hundred different smiles." Akash had laughed as he pulled her close.

"I need them. For all the different things I do." She shrugged one beautifully brown silky shoulder.

"What do you mean?"

She sat up on one elbow in bed, oblivious to the sheets and where they were. "For example. I have this one, for James. Friendly but he knows I'm the boss. And I have this one." She changed her expression to one of cool calm. "For when I want the board to wonder if I'm pissed off or what."

Akash laughed, thrilled to be getting this insight into this incredible woman.

"So..." He ran a finger over her shoulder and across her neck, enjoying the smoothness of her skin. "What smile do you have for me?" he asked. Why was he so needy around her?

"For you, I don't." She locked her eyes on to his. "What?"

"You get the real me. You get to see everything I'm feeling. No games. I hide nothing from you."

"Like right now, your smile says you want me to kiss you," he whispered.

"Then what are you waiting for?"

"Well, that's just it, isn't it?" Reena said softly, bringing him back down to earth. "Nothing worth having is ever easy."

Chapter Ten

"Mrs. Patel, I assure you that we have plenty of room for your family as well as the groom's." Reena promised the mother of the bride yet again. They had just been here two days ago. They were back again.

"Mom. Maybe we can have a smaller wedding. Just family?" Anu suggested.

"What did I tell you?" The mother of the bride held up her hand to shush her daughter. "I will handle this."

"But Mom—"

"But nothing." Mrs. Patel turned away from her daughter.

Reena opened her mouth, but Lalita interrupted. "Mrs. Patel, maybe I can get you and Anu some chai, and a snack. The bar is open."

Reena threw Lalita a look of gratitude. Handling an

overbearing mother was a delicate thing. She sighed as the three women headed for the bar, which doubled as a coffee shop, since the restaurant was currently closed due to lack of chef.

No sooner had Reena inhaled deeply to calm herself than loud voices from the front desk reached her. She hurried over and found one of the new trainees close to tears, as she typed away in the computer, while a guest yelled at her for not being able to find their reservation.

Upon seeing Reena, the look of panic in the woman's eyes increased and tears filled them. "Oh. Ms. Pandya. I'm so sorry—"

Reena was tight-lipped. She had seen this woman get flustered at the computer just the day before. If she didn't know how to use the computer, she should not be there. It was not her first day. Reena glanced around; there was no sign of Janki, the manager who was supposed to be mentoring her. Though Reena knew most of the staff she had been able to keep on did double or triple duty.

She moved closer to the woman, read her name tag. "Ishani?"

The guest was getting irritated and impatient. Never a good thing in the hotel business. "I have a reservation, and I expect a room."

"Of course. Ishani here—" Reena started.

"Appears to be incompetent."

Reena turned to Ishani, whose eyes were wide as she tapped away at the computer. A glance at the screen confirmed that the customer was indeed correct. Ishani wasn't even on the correct page. She never should have been left alone at the front desk.

Reena looked at Ishani. "Do you mind if I—?"

A relieved Ishani stepped back, gesturing at the computer. "Please." The woman eyed the customer warily.

Reena turned her attention to the customer. "Sir. Ishani is a new employee. Still training, and as such, I would ask that you be patient while we look up your reservation." Reena made a few clicks and brought up the desired information. "Here we go." Reena ran the keys and handed them to the customer. "I have upgraded your room at no cost and added a complimentary bottle of wine for your inconvenience."

The customer seemed placated and nodded at them both before leaving the desk.

Janki arrived just then. "Janki. Ishani. I'd like a word. In the back."

Both women followed her to the private office behind the check in area.

"I am not sure what happened out there, but it is clear to me that there is a level of inexperience that made it all the more difficult to deal with a tough client." Reena paused. "Janki, please work with Ishani until she gains proficiency with our systems. And Ishani, please take advantage of Janki's advice and experience."

"I am sorry, Ms. Pandya." Ishani spoke. "I'm really good on the computer, I'm just—"

"This is not the first time I have witnessed this. You don't need to make excuses. I need people who can do the job." Reena cut her off. Her phone buzzed. Maintenance had texted that there was some trouble with an AC unit. "I need to take care of this. You guys can get back to work." She left both women standing there, flushed and sheepish. Ishani looked relieved.

Chapter Eleven

Akash's Gupta Equity meeting had ended sooner than expected. He should have known. As long as his dad was able to increase the bottom line, nothing else mattered.

Akash had taken advantage of the time to get Anita Virani on the phone. She was very excited about the idea of a work retreat. Most of the partners at JFL were family, but they were growing and had a number of associate lawyers, as well as staff whom she felt would benefit from a retreat.

"That sounds like a really great idea. I'm so glad you called me about this! Let's go ahead and book this one year and see how it goes. If the event is well received, and the venue works out for our group, we'd be happy to book in the future."

"Of course—you won't be disappointed. I can assure you that."

"Listen. I know Reena is struggling over there—Sangeeta is my husband's cousin. So I'll give you a heads-up. The entire Joshi family are foodies. You have good food—we're sold. Oh, and a spa would be amazing. Although that's my personal preference. But what lawyer doesn't need a massage?" She laughed.

"Thanks for the tip, Anita. Appreciate it. When do you want this to happen?"

He heard her typing as she pulled up her calendar. "Charlotte handles our scheduling and events, but it looks like we have a long weekend in early November. I'll just email her to confirm, and then you'll be dealing with her."

Excitement shot through his body. She was talking about the same weekend as the Shah Wedding. Whatever. This was a start. All they had to do was impress them, and then Lulu's would be their retreat destination moving forward. It was just the beginning.

"Excellent, Anita."

He had started to text Reena the fabulous news when he remembered that while they might be working together, they weren't together. This was information that could wait until he saw his *business partner* again.

Since he still had some time, he stopped off to see Asha. He took the elevator to the penthouse, the doors opening directly into her foyer. He entered the apartment only to find Kirti and his mom there. He nearly got back on the elevator to go down when Asha saw him.

"Don't you dare leave, Bhaiya." Asha was firm. Huh. She was feeling better.

He inhaled. "Wouldn't dream of it."

He walked over and hugged her, nodding to his mom, who was cooking. The aromas were familiar and brought back happy feelings from his childhood.

Pre-divorce.

He inhaled deeply the scent of onions, garlic and tomato frying. He caught Kirti's eye and nodded a greeting to her as well. "You back to work?" he asked Asha. He smiled. "All those minds to influence on TikTok."

She shook her head. "No. I'm going back to school. After all this, I decided not to put my life on display anymore. It's fabulous when things are good, but when things go bad....well I wish I didn't have to share all that."

"You have actually been an inspiration, Asha Ben." Kirti spoke up. She pulled out her phone. "Look at this." She approached them both, Asha's TikTok feed on her phone. "All these comments of support. People love that you want to go back to school. They are inspired by your journey."

Asha shook her head. "Look at that comment. So mean."

"Haters gonna hate," Akash said in unison with Kirti. They met each other's eyes. She was as surprised as he was that they agreed on something.

"You think I should keep this up?" Asha looked at him with surprise. "I always thought you thought this was flighty."

"Not at all. You could really be a positive influence

on people. Watching you get up and reinvent yourself—
it's amazing." Akash was serious. "Where's Nila?"

"Out with Priya—again." Asha smirked. "If you're
not careful, our little Nila may get married before either of us."

"I would so love to plan a wedding," their mother
quipped from the kitchen.

Akash shook his head. "It won't be mine."

"Seriously, Bhaiya? You're not seeing anyone?"

"No."

"Huh." Asha grinned. "Nila and I were sure you
were seeing someone. You were really weird and hard
to reach for a few months."

What?

Surely he hadn't been that obvious when he and
Reena were together, had he? Akash plastered on his
most innocent face and shook his head. "What do you
mean weird?"

"You smiled more, got irritated less. And you were
always running off to some 'meeting.'" Asha shrugged.
"We assumed you had a girlfriend and weren't ready
to share yet."

"Nope." He looked away from her. His sisters were
more perceptive than he'd given them credit for.

"You're not getting younger," his mother joked from
the kitchen.

"Since when do you care, Jaymini," he mumbled.

His mother stopped what she was doing and came
around to where he stood. She lifted her chin to him.
He stood at least a head over her, but the emotion in
her tone took him off-balance. "I am your mother. You

may be angry about things that happened in the past, but you will stop disrespecting me by calling me by first name. Don't call me mom if you don't want, but you will not call me Jaymini." Her eyes blazed with power at him, her voice was low but firm, the way he got when he was angry. She wielded her mother card with the power of a parent that no child ever outgrows. "I have let your insolence slide too long. You want to be angry." She frowned as she shrugged one shoulder. "Be angry. But do it on your own time."

Akash swallowed hard, heat rising to his face, suddenly very aware of his sisters around him, mortified to have been called out for his behavior, at the age of thirty, by his mother.

"You left us." He sounded weak and needy, even to himself.

She shook her head. "No. I left your father. I *never left you.*"

"You didn't even fight for us." Tears burned behind his eyes, and his voice cracked at his words.

"That. Is. BS. Of course I fought for you. Your father had more resources than me. And he had the gall to fight me back. The courts decided that since he was financially better off, you three lived with him. I was granted visitation."

"That's not true."

"I am many things, Akash. But a liar is not one of them." She met his gaze firmly. Same dark eyes as his own. "I came to get you children every chance I had. Your sisters came—you refused. I couldn't force you to come with me." Her eyes softened. "Maybe I should have. I was the adult—I knew that you needed your mother, even if you were angry."

"You didn't see how heartbroken dad was. You didn't see what you did to him," Akash said.

"What I did to him? Are you serious?" She glanced at Asha. "You never told him?"

"Told him what, Mom?" Asha looked completely baffled.

His mother glanced at Kirti, who shook her head at her. "You didn't tell your sisters?" his mom asked Kirti.

"It wasn't my place to tell," Kirti said. "And I was afraid they wouldn't believe me. I loved having sisters, and I didn't want to ruin that."

"Tell us what?" Akash looked at Asha. She was as baffled as he was.

"Why I left."

"Why did you leave?" Akash asked as the elevator door swooshed open. Nila came out, looking ravishing in a long flowing summer dress. It wasn't often that Nila wore a dress. Asha must be right; things were getting serious between Nila and Priya.

"Hi, Bhaiya." She hugged him. "How's the hotel?"

"Fine. How's Priya?" He raised an eyebrow.

His baby sister flushed, and he realized she wasn't his baby sister anymore. A part of him was joyous and a part of him was sad. "She's awesome."

"Hey, Kirti." She looked between the two of them. "Wow, you two in the same room." She widened her eyes. "And both still alive. Impressive."

She seemed oblivious of the tension in the room. Or likely, she didn't care. She moved to the kitchen and reached into one of the pots with a spoon. "Why does everyone look so serious?" she asked, her mouth full of dhal.

"Mom was just going to tell us why she left," Asha said.

Nila furrowed her brow. "You guys don't know?"

Akash raised his eyebrows. "You do?"

"He cheated." Nila ate dhal and rice she had taken out for herself as if she hadn't just dropped a bomb.

"He what?" Akash couldn't believe it. He had watched his father fall apart when his mother left.

"Dad cheated on Mom," Nila repeated.

"How do you know, and they don't?" their mother asked, waving a finger at Akash and Asha.

"I heard you talking to Rakesh Uncle one night when you thought we were sleeping." Nila shrugged. "Actually made sense once I knew. I figured I was the last to know, being the youngest, but—ha! Look at that, I knew something before you two." Her eyes widened with her victory.

"You didn't tell us?" Asha's eyes widened, aghast.

"I thought you two probably already knew. Kirti and I found out at the same time. Adults always underestimate their kids. They thought we were sleeping, but we heard." Nila shrugged.

Akash's heart was racing; there was a buzzing in his ears. "No. That can't be. If that was true, you could have used that to get custody."

"I couldn't prove it. Your father cheated more than once. He was always sorry, but after a time, I couldn't take it anymore. I left."

But everything he remembered was his father doting on his mother….and his mother crying.

"All those times he brought presents, hired help, took you on vacation—"

His mother tightened her lips. "Guilt and apologies. He was sorry. It would never happen again." She paused. "It always did. I couldn't take it anymore. I still loved him, I loved you three but his infidelity… I deserved better."

Akash's head was spinning. He had no idea how to process all this. He looked at Nila and Asha. Nila was calm, but Asha shared his confusion.

Asha moved first. She crossed the room and hugged their mother. "Mom. I'm so sorry you went through all that. And good for you for standing up for yourself. It must have been so hard."

"I'm so glad you found out about Rahul before you married him." His mother hugged his sister. "You deserve better. The worst was having to leave you three. I had believed that I would get custody, after I went to school and got my degree. But social work just doesn't compare in income to buying and selling businesses." She sighed. "And the truth was, by then I was afraid that if I did get custody, he would cut you off financially. I didn't want that to happen, to take away opportunities that were available to you. But I was always thrilled with our weekends and our calls." She glanced at Nila as she joined the hug. "We did okay, huh? The rest is all past."

But it wasn't all past for Akash. "All these years, I thought… I was so angry… Why didn't you tell me?"

"Tell you that your hero was a cheater?" His mother shook her head. "No. You love your father. He has *some* good qualities. He was a bad husband."

"All this time… I thought you had abandoned…" It was too much. Maybe the girls could forgive and forget; he could not. He caught Kirti's eye. She watched him, her expression blank.

"I can't do this right now." He left.

Just three months ago, Akash had opened the door to the aroma of burnt food and the sound of eighties music playing. His heart lightened. He hadn't expected Reena at his place that day. He took off his shoes and quietly walked into the main area.

Reena's hair was down and she was belting out an old heavy metal song, about sugar being poured, using a belan as a microphone. He stood and watched her shake her adorably sexy behind, before she bent over and flicked her head and hair in front of her, then stood, flicking her hair back, all while she sang badly.

Akash undid his tie, and unbuttoned and untucked his shirt, grabbed a ladle and joined her. Her eyes popped open when she saw him, but she did not miss a beat, and they sang and danced together until the end of the song.

She dropped her belan in the sink and hugged him. "Rough day?"

"How did you know?"

She pulled back, her arms around his neck. "I see your sister almost every day. She mentioned it."

"Asha?"

"Nila."

"Really? Need to watch the quiet ones." He chuck-led. "Is that why you're here?"

She pursed her lips. "Maaybe. Also, I missed you."

"I saw you two days ago."

"Are you saying that you did not miss me?" She raised an eyebrow.

"No. I'm saying why did it take forty-eight hours before you missed me?" He tightened his grip and laughed, knowing she would attempt to squirm away.

And she did. But she ended up laughing. "I tried to make khichdi."

He nodded. "I smell the attempt."

She kissed him. "No worries, I ran to my brother's, and got some of his."

Akash stared at her. "Thank god for The Masala Hut."

She stepped back. "Let's eat." She scooped out the khichdi into two bowls, and set them on the table, where the papad, spicy pickle, ghee and yogurt were already placed.

Akash looked at the table and he felt his body relax. Reena sat down, and he sat beside her.

"Tell me what happened," she said as they started to eat.

The khichdi was warm and comforting. He told her the story. His father's latest merger would cost jobs to one hundred and twenty-five people. "He feels it's up to the two companies to deal with the losses, not his."

"You disagree."

"I always have." He added more spicy pickle to

his bowl and took another bite. "Your brother is an amazing cook."

Reena had beamed as she nodded her agreement. She didn't have makeup on, her hair was tousled and she was wearing oversize sweats and a T-shirt. She was drop dead gorgeous.

They finished eating, and Reena led him to the window where they stood in the dark and watched the city at night. She wrapped her arms around him. "I believe in you. You'll find something for those people."

He wrapped his arms around her. Her body fit perfectly with his. She smelled of the flowery shampoo she kept at his place, and that indescribable something that was uniquely Reena.

His agitation from the day was gone. He'd deal with his father again tomorrow. But today, right now, he was in Reena's arms.

He was home.

Akash left Asha's penthouse and walked, all the new information swirling around in his head. He thought about Reena and craved her comfort, but it was lost to him. He'd never get it back. He had a place to live, but he was a man without a home.

Chapter Twelve

Reena met with maintenance, giving the okay to pur-
chase a new AC unit. Whatever that was going to cost,
it had to be done. This one had been on its last leg for
the past year. She gave thanks for once to the money
from Gupta Equity. She may not be happy about how
she got it, but she supposed she had to acknowledge the
reality of the situation at last—that money was keeping her afloat. She headed back to her suite, changed
her clothes and reheated some leftovers.

Honestly though, the day she'd had. New AC unit.
Challenges at the front desk. No luck in the search for
chef. Not to mention dealing with Akash every. Single.
Minute. Of the day. Her phone buzzed. Her mom. She
let it buzz again while she debated answering. She did
not have the energy for this. She caved. "Hey, Mom."

She sat down on the sofa with her food and placed her phone on speaker.

"Hi, Beti. What's going on with the AC unit?"

How did she know already? Reena had literally had this conversation with maintenance an hour ago. "It's fine. I took care of it."

"You can't just go around buying new equipment. Lulu's does not have that kind of money," her mother said.

Reena rolled her eyes. "I am aware of what Lulu's has. But we won't get weddings and meetings if the AC doesn't work. We've needed a new one for a couple of years already. This one has had it. So I gave Mr. Cole authorization to buy a new one."

"With what money?"

Reena paused, and put down her bowl of dhal and rice, her appetite gone. "You were there when we signed the papers."

"You mean the Gupta money? Well of course. But you can't use that money." Her mother stated this as if it were fact.

"Why not? The whole point of the agreement was to be able to use that money. Otherwise why give fifty-one percent to them?" Reena riled up.

"Honestly, Reena. Using that money—"

"What would you have me do? The bank would have taken Lulu's. At least this way, we still have Lulu's in the family." Leave it to her mother to force her to defend Akash and his money.

"Stretched out the AC use."

Reena literally face-palmed in frustration. "Mom.

We have a wedding in a few weeks. Then we have another huge wedding a few weeks after that. September, October, and even November are highly unpredictable in terms of weather. We need the AC."

"It could have gone another year."

Reena inhaled. Her mother was only being unreasonable because she blamed Reena for putting them in a position to have to use someone else's money.

Jaya Pandya had not even allowed Reena to borrow clothes and jewelry from her girlfriends when she growing up.

"We provide for you. That should be enough." She would say. Reena stood by while the other girls traded clothes and makeup like sisters, while she sat to one side and watched.

To her mother, using the Gupta money was simply an extension of that. A reminder that they could not provide for themselves. A reminder to Reena of her failure.

Her mother was still talking. Barking orders like Reena was an incompetent employee. "Now make sure you have a minimum requirement for the room block—"

There was a knock at her door. Odd. But perfectly timed. "I have to go, Mom. Love you, bye!" Reena had learned about minimum room blocks when she was ten years old. It was her mother who had taught her. She certainly did not need a reminder.

She got off the sofa, placed her bowl in the small sink and headed for the door. She peeked through the small hole, and her heart thudded in her chest.

What the hell was he doing here?

* * *

Reena opened the door to him, her hair up in a messy bun, wearing his old University of Maryland T-shirt. Akash could tell, though, that something was bothering her—her jaw was set and her defenses were clearly up.

But his heart ached, and the sight of her was a balm to his turmoil. "My dad cheated on my mom. That's why she left." Akash blurted the words out as if they were poisoning him from the inside. Maybe they were.

Her eyes softened immediately, and she reached out her hand and he took it, allowing her to let him into her suite. The door shut behind him with a soft click.

Her lemon ginger scent permeated everything in this room and everything fell away but her. His hand was still in hers, so without thinking, he pulled her to him and leaned in to Reena and kissed her. To his great satisfaction, she allowed it, and she kissed him back. Her body next to his was warm and soft and she pressed against him as she intensified their kiss.

She smelled amazing. His body reacted immediately to the familiarity of her. To her scent, to her warmth, to the way she kissed him with abandon. He gave in to everything he'd wanted and missed.

He had been denied this comfort for too long by his own actions. Right now, he couldn't even remember why he had let her go.

He pressed his mouth to hers and she opened for him. He kissed her, roughly, full of need and frustration, and she matched him. He lifted her up and she immediately wrapped her legs around his waist, her mouth never leaving his.

He carried her to the bedroom, holding her in his arms, staring at her as they stood next to her bed.

She pulled back and smirked at him. "Just drop me."

"You're wearing my UMD T-shirt."

She looked up at him from under her lashes. "So drop me and take it off."

"You're the boss." He said and removed his hands from her bottom just as she let go of his neck.

She landed on her back, the smirk still on her face. "You can take off this T-shirt, but you're not taking it home."

He unbuttoned his shirt and she peeled it from his body. He pulled the soft T-shirt over her head and joined her on the bed, his mouth on her neck. This was Reena. His best source of comfort. He relished the feel of her skin on his. His heart had brought him here. He was lost, but right now, with her body against his, her arms around him, he was found.

There was no thought, only doing, feeling, loving. He captured her in his arms and she pushed him so she was on top of him.

Reena didn't want to think about what was happening. Akash had showed up at her room hurt, wounded. She instinctually had wanted to cure his pain, take care of his emotional wounds.

In the next instant, Akash's mouth had been on hers, and her body took over. They never had been able to quite get enough of each other.

She caught his eye, as she straddled him on the bed, his face full of hurt and desire.

"How did you find out?" She asked.

"Nila."

"Nila knew?" Maybe he just needed to talk.

"Not now, Reena. I can't talk right now." He effortlessly pulled himself up and kissed her, his arms enveloping her the way he knew she loved.

All thoughts of conversation left her mind. She allowed herself to become completely consumed with Akash and what was happening between them. She shut off that part of her mind that was asking what the hell was happening, the part that reminded her that *he* had been the one to leave *her*. For a split second that part of her brain dominated, warning her that nothing had changed and she would regret this in the morning.

Then Akash put his mouth on her throat, and his hands on her bottom, removing her sweatpants and she gave into her need. She wanted this, she wanted *him*, consequences be damned.

Hours later, they lay side by side on her bed, spent and sated. The only sound, the sound of their breathing. Heavy but slowly evening out.

He needed to leave. Reena could not even risk a glance at him. This shouldn't have happened. What had seemed obvious and comforting a few hours ago was now unbelievable in the harsh actuality of the real world.

He had made it abundantly clear he didn't want to be

with her. And she had no interest in being with some-one who had no faith in her.

"You should go."

"I should go."

They spoke at the same time.

"Right." They said once again in unison.

It didn't make sense, nor was it fair, but the fact that he wanted to leave, hurt her more than it should, given she really needed him to leave.

She pulled the sheets tighter over her body, suddenly self-conscious. She continued to stare at the ceiling and steeled her voice. "Your sister lives just down the hall. Just FYI."

"She's not really my sister." His voice changed at the end into something like anguish. Reena snapped her head over to him, but he was already sitting up, his muscular, bronzed back to her. She had the sudden urge to touch him again. To pull him back to her. But this time, that part of her brain that protected her won out, and she kept her hands to herself. He turned his pro-file to her, as if he wanted to say something, but didn't.

"She may not be your sister. But you knew who I was talking about."

He turned away from her and quickly dressed. She tried not to watch. She had enjoyed watching him dress when they'd been together. Something about watching him dress in the morning had been as exciting as re-moving his clothes at night.

She was still in love with him. She knew it. If she had only felt lust for him while they had been together, she would have been able to resist him tonight. She would never have been able to put her own hurt aside to soothe him. But that was what she had done.

Her heart ached with the reality of her feelings. All this time, she had leaned into her anger because anger was easy, defined and almost expected.

Love was none of those things.

It was suddenly very clear to her. He did not love her enough to trust her, so she would never be with him.

He threw his tie around his neck and left without either of them saying another word.

Reena had been completely enjoying herself at the hotelier conference in Vegas; it was fascinating. She loved everything about the hotel business. Providing comfort, a home away from home, a luxurious get-away with every detail attended to. The conference was informative and challenging, but after a long day of learning and networking, all she wanted was a glass of wine, a chapter of her book and her bed.

She was enjoying her standard white wine at the bar when a few men from her conference came and sat a few stools away from her. They ordered many rounds of drinks, and became increasingly loud and obnox-ious, finally turning their attention to her.

She ignored the first couple of passes. Her experi-ence had told her that these guys were basically harm-less and ignoring them usually meant they would go away.

Then one of them approached her. Great, she had thought. Her first instinct was to down her wine and take her book upstairs. But then she got pissed. She should be able to sit there and enjoy her book without running from ridiculous men, so she stayed put.

The man reeked of alcohol and could barely even get his pathetic line out. She firmly told him she wasn't interested. But he was not to be deterred. He insisted she let him buy her a drink. She refused. He did it anyway.

She had turned to him, boiling with indignation, ready to give him a piece of her mind, when an excessively handsome man approached from behind the drunk.

"There you are, sweetheart." The handsome man had come and stood by her, hovering his hand at the small of her back. "I'm so sorry. The meeting ran late. I know we said drinks, but why don't we just go to bed?"

Reena was not the type of woman to be swept away, nor was she the type to need saving, but he smelled like chocolate-chip cookies and he was fabulous to look at. Not to mention, the word bed *coming out of his perfect lips made her flush like a schoolgirl, even though he wasn't suggesting anything.*

The handsome man towered a head and muscles over the jerk. He turned to the jerk. "She's with me."

The jerk slithered away.

As soon as the jerk was gone, the handsome man removed his hand, and offered it to her in handshake. "Akash Gupta."

She had stared at his hand. "What the hell was that?"

"I thought you were in trouble. I was getting that jerk to leave you alone." He had furrowed his brow in

surprise. Was she supposed to fall at his feet in grati-tude?

"I can handle myself, thank you very much," she had snapped.

"You're welcome," he had snapped back.

"I didn't thank you."

"I know."

"I didn't need saving. Honestly, men are either jerks like that guy or idiots like you."

"I am not an idiot. I was trying to help—"

"I didn't ask for it."

"Noted. Well, enjoy your evening," he had said curtly and then left.

The next night, drained and exhausted again, Reena walked into the bar with her book, and ordered her wine. She enjoyed a peaceful hour reading and sip-ping before deciding to call it a night.

She asked for the bill and was told by the bartender that it had been taken care of. He nodded behind her and she turned to find Akash standing there, looking ridiculously handsome and contrite.

He put his hands out in defense. "Before you go off on me, let me say that I bought your drink as a peace offering. I'm not hitting on you. Or helping you. Or whatever. You were right. I should have minded my own business."

She couldn't help smiling. "Actually, I was thinking that maybe I had been too hard on you."

His grin widened. "You were?"

She nodded. Neither of them moved.

"Would you want to have a drink with me?" he asked.

"Sure." She motioned to the stool next to her. *"Reena Pandya."*

She enjoyed a drink with him, and conversation came easy. Akash was intelligent and kind and big-hearted and easy to talk to. They moved to the comfy chairs and continued talking until the bar closed.

The next night, Reena entered the bar telling herself that she wasn't looking for Akash. She'd brought her book to prove it. No sooner had she ordered her white wine than she felt him come sit next to her.

"I told myself I wasn't coming here to find you," he said, his deep voice soft and low, for only her to hear. *"But I lied."*

She grinned and turned to him. "I'm not looking for a relationship."

"Neither am I."

The bartender brought her wine. She chugged it, and then turned to him, one eyebrow raised. He motioned for her to lead the way. By the time the elevator doors opened on her floor, she had her tongue down his throat and his hands were under her skirt.

Chapter Thirteen

"A kash! Is that you?" Kirti's voice startled him just as he stepped away from Reena's closed door. She was holding a card key, so she was clearly coming home.

Oh crap. He hadn't even bothered to button his dress shirt over his undershirt. His tie was draped around his neck. His hair was tousled from Reena running her fingers through and grabbing it. There was no doubt as to what he had been doing in her room.

There was also no avoiding his stepsister. "Hey."

"Hey?" Her eyes widened. "You just stepped out of Reena's room, looking like you—looking...*rumpled*, and all you can say is hey?"

Silence was the best option here. Kirti watched him, expectantly. She looked from the door to him and back.

"I need to go," Akash said and started on his way.

"Wait," Kirti yelled to him.

"No," he called over his shoulder and kept walking.

"You're sleeping with her," she cried out.

He walked back to her, so she wouldn't do that again.

"No. I am not sleeping with her." He had *slept* with her. It would not happen again.

"Don't lie to me. I can see what happened here." Kirti eyed the door, clearly uncomfortable with this knowledge.

"Whatever. Quite frankly, it's none of your—or anyone else's—business." He stared her in the eye to make himself clear. She was not to tell anyone what she suspected. "So don't tell anyone."

Kirti smirked. "I make no promises." She walked away in the opposite direction and waved. "Sleep well." She chuckled.

There was no sleep for him at all the rest of that night. Between his encounter with Kirti, his new found knowledge of his father's infidelities, and the amazing evening in Reena's bed, his mind and body would not quiet. He tossed and turned all night.

Akash woke groggy, and coffee would not fill the void. What he really needed was chai. To that end, he found himself at The Masala Hut, in line with the rest of Baltimore, trying to get a cup of chai.

Akash barely knew Reena's brother Sonny, who owned the place, but he'd had his chai more than once when Reena would jog over and get it.

When his order was ready he took his drink over to

one of the tables by the window, sat down and opened his laptop, trying to lose himself in his work.

"My brother makes the best chai—I told you." Reena's voice, low and quiet, interrupted him and he looked up to find her sipping her own chai. She was clad in running gear. Sweaty. And oh so sexy.

He swallowed hard. "You were correct." Keep it formal. He didn't need to think about the fact that she had been naked in his arms just hours ago.

"I'm correct about many things." She sat down across from him as she drank her chai.

"Just one thing I did not mention about JFL—they all love food. Anita indicated the best way to get them was through their stomachs." He glanced at the back. "Your brother…?"

Reena shook her head. "No. I've already made him do one too many things, and he really wants to focus on growing his business here. But that's fine. We have three chef interviews today."

Akash snapped his head to her. He had forgotten.

"It's okay if you're busy. I can handle it."

"No. I'll be there. I just haven't looked at my schedule yet." He avoided her eyes.

"The Patel bride has two cousins, close in age. One engaged, wants to marry next year. The other about to get engaged. If we make this family happy, then we're set with a few weddings coming up."

She was talking like they were partners.

They were partners. At least in business.

They sat together quietly—awkwardly—for a few

minutes, sipping chai together. He desperately tried to come up with something to say.

"Um so… Kirti did see me leaving last night," Akash blurted, then raised his head and met Reena's gaze.

"I told you to be careful." Reena glared at him.

"I walked out of your room and there she was. It's not like I could ignore her. I told her not to say anything."

"Will she listen?" Her eyebrows raised.

"She hates me, so probably not." Akash shrugged.

Reena stared at him a moment. "Whatever. It's not like it will ever happen again, right?"

"Of course not. That would be foolish. I broke up with you."

"Uh, excuse me. I broke up with you, too," Reena shot back at him.

"When?" Akash was astonished.

"When you decided you did not have faith in my ability to save my own hotel and had discussions about giving Lulu's money, behind my back," Reena hissed at him.

Right.

"Anyway, I just came over to see how you were doing. About your dad."

"I don't know." He shrugged. "Pissed."

"You really looked up to him." Her whole face softened again.

He stared at her. "I've been misled before."

She clenched her jaw as she stood. "You know what, fine. I came over to check on you. Clearly that was a mistake." She fired a look at him. "Just like last night. It won't happen again."

He nodded at her. "Of course." He knew where that led. Long nights in each other's arms. Someone to come home to. Someone to disappoint you. Someone whose lack of presence makes you physically hurt.

She stared at him with those hazel eyes that had always appeared to look right through him, saying nothing. He was positive she was reading his mind. "It always leads us to somewhere we don't belong."

Standing, she picked up her precious chai and walked away.

Chapter Fourteen

Reena had hoped her brother's chai would help fuel her, but she had finished her chai, and the confrontation with Akash had drained her of energy. She walked back to the kitchen, her heart heavy and her brain mush.

One thing was becoming abundantly clear.

She and Akash Gupta were complete chaos.

They had started as a hookup in Vegas, after all. How could they possibly ever have been in anything that even resembled real relationship?

Akash Gupta was a distraction from her goals. She was better off without him.

Last night was a fluke.

Not that Reena would know a real relationship if it had hit her in the face. She had dated, had some "long-term" boyfriends. But those things usually ended after a few months. When she and Akash had hit the six-month mark, it had been a milestone for both of them.

She had thought he was the one. The other guys (boys, really) never understood what her work meant to her. Marriage, being in a relationship, having her own family, these were things that had never been a priority for her. Not until she met Akash.

Akash had seemed to understand her passion for success from day one. In fact, it had seemed to her that the harder she worked, the deeper their bond became.

Or so she had thought. Until he lost faith in her and decided to fund Lulu's behind her back. And then broke up with her over Asha's wedding. Or nonwedding.

Reena had already met the chefs they were interviewing today. She simply needed to review their files in preparation of the tasting portion of the interview later today.

First, though, she needed to talk to her brother in person. She missed him. Sure he had called the other day, to warn her about their mother's call, but she wanted to see him in person.

She walked into the kitchen holding her empty to-go mug. She stayed in the doorway since Sonny was a stickler for the health code. Though she was sure even standing in the doorway was prohibited. The aromas of spicy paratha, dabeli and pani puri made her stomach growl. But for her, it was always chai first. Then food.

Her brother was a study in efficiency and grace. He was made to run a kitchen and he did it well. He glanced over his shoulder and saw her standing there.

His lips were pressed together, but she saw relief in his eyes. She waited.

After a few minutes, his second chef Dharm took over, Sonny removed his apron, washed his hands and nodded to the door that led to the hallway and his office. She went through it, him behind her.

Sonny was only a year and half older than her, but he'd practically raised her and Jai while their parents worked to build Lulu's. It was Sonny who made them dinner, Sonny who had helped with homework. He was more than just her big brother.

He closed his office door. "Hey."

"How long are you going to be mad at me?" she asked.

"I'm not mad—I just don't know who you are." He leaned against his desk.

"I was doing what was right for the hotel." She defended herself.

"At the expense of another person. A friend." His voice was gentle, but the reprimand was loud and clear.

"A client."

"Why is that different?" Sonny shook his head at her.

"I was never going to let her marry him," she said softly.

Sonny crossed his arms across his chest. "Really? How would that help you?"

Reena sighed. Wasn't it obvious? "I was going to let all the guests arrive, stay at the hotel, see how amazing it is. Then I would have confronted him the day before the wedding. Asha would have cancelled. Boom. Done. She doesn't marry a louse. I get my hotel."

Her brother just stared at her. Then he shook his head at her. "Unbelievable."

"What?" How was that not understandable? Everyone got where they needed to be and she did not lose the hotel. She didn't fail.

"Honestly, Reena, I love you. But you have lost your way."

"I have not. Men do this all the time. And no one calls them out." Reena pouted. "Mom would have done the same thing."

Sonny nodded his head. "You're correct. Men do that kind of thing all the time. And quite frankly, so do women—maybe no one calls them out." He stepped closer to her. "That doesn't make it right. You're better than that. The Reena I grew up with was not only a kick-ass businessperson but she cared about people. And the fact that Mom would have done the same thing should scare you."

"Hey! I need my chai fix." Sangeeta came bounding in the office and halted when she saw Reena with Sonny. "Oop. Sorry." She made to leave.

Sonny turned to her, and his face lit up. "Don't go." He went to her and took her hand. "I haven't seen you in days."

Sangeeta flushed. "I saw you for lunch."

"That was thirty-six hours ago."

It was time for Reena to leave. These two were saccharin sweet and it was painful to watch.

"I'll see you later." She started to get past them.

"You missed Sunday dinner last night," Sonny said. "Come next time?"

She had her brother back. She nearly teared up. "Yes."

"Two weeks. Don't be late."

"You got it." She looked at Sangeeta. "I'll see you later today?"

"Absolutely."

Reena left. She refreshed her chai on the way out, feeling a bit lighter, now that Sonny was talking to her again. She didn't understand what he was getting at. He did not understand her nearly as much as she thought he had.

Chapter Fifteen

Akash finished his emails and refilled his chai before leaving The Masala Hut and going to his father's
apartment. Thoughts and images of Reena from last
night had interrupted his concentration, so it had taken
longer than usual to get through the morning emails.

It wasn't quite nine in the morning, so his father
would still be working from home. Akash let himself
into his father's condo. He found his father the way he
usually did. Postworkout, at the computer, glasses on,
deep in concentration. Akash held his chai to-go mug
in front of him, like a shield. As if it gave him strength.

"Tell me why mom left." Akash stood in front of
his father. He didn't bother with the pleasantries. That
wasn't their dynamic.

His father looked up at him. Something about him

made his father sit back from his computer and take off his glasses. "What?"

"You heard me. I never asked, but I'm asking now." Akash stood firm, despite the butterflies in his stomach.

"You know. She told you." His father had the gall to appear upset at this.

"No. She did not tell me."

"Then why are you asking?"

"I want to know. From you." He half-expected his father to say he wasn't going to answer any such questions, but instead, he took off his glasses and sighed, looking suddenly much older than his fifty-seven years.

"I was an idiot." He sighed. "There were...women."

"More than one?"

His father's shoulders sagged. Akash seemed to notice for the first time, the graying at his temples, the wrinkles at his eyes and maybe the fact that he appeared thinner than usual.

"Yes, but what does it matter how many? It only takes one to hurt your marriage...and the woman you love." He looked out the window and the city bathed in midmorning sunshine. "She found out, of course and we argued, and I swore I would never look at another woman again. Then I would take you all on some fabulous vacation, rekindle that spark with your mother. And things would be good for a while. Until I slipped up again. And again. Even when she left, I didn't really get it. How much I'd hurt her." He sighed. "But now, I see how terrible I was to her. How disrespectful to our marriage. Not a day goes by that I don't regret it." He pressed his lips together. "Too little, too late. Rakesh loves your mother as she deserves."

"That's it?" Akash was fuming.

"What do you mean? You mother forgave me many times, and I still broke my promises to her. She left. Found happiness. I'm not asking for sympathy or even forgiveness. I was an idiot and I lost the best person in my life."

"You fought her for custody."

"I was hurt, irrational and I had power and money. So I used it. Another regret. I tried to make up for it by letting you all spend as much time with each other as you wanted."

"You let me hate her all these years." Akash leaned across the desk, his voice rising. He never raised his voice, and now he'd done it twice in two days.

"No, I didn't."

"You most certainly did. I felt bad for you, that's why I never wanted to leave you and go to Mom's. I thought she left...she left..." He started pacing at his father's denial.

"You thought she left you?"

"I was a kid. What was I supposed to think? Then I heard you talking to Kaka. Saying how you had provided for her, and she left anyway." He walked back and forth in front of his father's desk, all his emotions coming back to the surface. He was eight years old, and his mother had just left him.

"I threw money at her out of guilt. I was not a good man." His father sat and watched him pace.

Fury moved his legs and pounded his heart. He'd

spent his life idolizing his father and being angry with his mother. He was a complete idiot. His father did not deserve his adulation, any more than his mother deserved his anger.

Chapter Sixteen

Reena showered and changed into her cream suit before making her way to her office to catch up on emails and phone calls. At noon, she went down to the restaurant. She had left her hair down today for a change. According to Sangeeta, doing a tight ponytail every day was bad for your hair. She had rolled her eyes when Sangeeta had mentioned it, but the truth was, Reena had no sisters, or even close girlfriends who would know and tell her these things. So deep down, she appreciated the advice.

She entered the restaurant to find Akash waiting for her. Well, he wasn't waiting for *her*, he was waiting to get started. She calmed her ridiculous nerves and put on her ice princess face. That's what Jai called it. It was really just her resting bitch face.

Reena had set up a cooking challenge of sorts to narrow down her choice of chef. These three chefs looked great on paper, but the real test would be their food.

She nodded at Akash. "Thanks for joining me." He was dressed in another beautifully cut suit, jacket open, no tie.

"Of course." He seemed agitated.

"You okay?" she whispered. Though she wasn't sure why she cared, or why she was whispering.

"I saw my dad," he whispered back. Akash stood and removed his jacket, and sat down, rolling up his sleeves as James brought out the courses.

"Want to talk about it?" she asked, only slightly distracted by his corded forearms. She held her phone tight to keep from trailing her fingers across them.

"Not right now." He motioned to James, who was waiting to get started.

They began with appetizers, then moved to main courses. The appetizers showcased each chef's creativity, and all three were wonderful. For the main course, Reena had requested a simple dhal-and-rice dish.

"Just dhal and rice?" Akash asked. "You didn't want to try the chicken curry or their bindi?" He asked in a singsong voice, as he tried to tempt her with her favorites.

She leaned close to him, nearly whispering in his ear. She was so close to him their breaths could mingle. "If they can make a fabulous dhal and rice, they can make anything."

Akash turned to face her, and his mouth nearly grazed hers. She swallowed hard as her breath came fast, and her heart thudded in her chest. She forced herself to pull back a few inches. He cleared his throat. "Right. Um. Makes sense."

They tried the dhal and rice of each chef to disappointing results. Reena went through the motions of trying the sweets they had made, but she knew her search was not quite over.

"Thank you all for your efforts." Reena stood. "James will be in touch."

"Thank you." Akash stood. "James, there seem to be plenty of leftovers. With Ms. Pandya's permission, maybe the staff could enjoy a meal?" He looked at Reena.

"Fantastic idea." She glanced at her assistant. "Please see to it that none of the food is wasted."

"Of course."

She exited the restaurant with Akash at her heels. "Thoughts?"

"I like the apps. The dhal and rice of chef number two was—"

"Completely bland!"

"I know. Did he put any masala in it at all? It was like the luchko dhal my mom used to give the girls when they were babies." He chuckled.

Reena chuckled, too. "My thoughts exactly. Chef three showed some promise."

"But you don't want to compromise." Akash's voice was soft and buttery right now, as they tried not to be heard.

"Exactly. I'm happy to give Ginger and Cardamom

my business until I get the right person to run that kitchen."

"Speaking of Ginger and Cardamom, I spoke with Amar Virani. He says they were never booked for the day-of food for Asha. As in, no deposit, no concrete menu." Akash's brow was furrowed. "Why would that be?"

Her heart thudded in her chest. "How would I know? I wasn't their planner." But she did know. It was because she, herself had cancelled them, knowing that Asha would never be getting married. "How did it go with your dad?" She couldn't help herself. He was hurting.

He gave a one-shouldered shrug. "He didn't deny it. He regrets it, but he has moved on."

She rested a hand on his arm. "I'm sorry. That has to, well, really suck." She bit her bottom lip as they stood there like that and she debated hugging him.

Thankfully, Akash's phone buzzed just then. "Sorry I need to take this." He put his phone to his ear, and she nodded at him and headed for the main lobby.

Kirti was waiting for her, as well as Anu, without her mother.

She approached Anu first. The young woman was wringing her hands, clearly agitated. "I'm so sorry I'm late," Reena started. "Things are…well, busy. Getting ready for your big day." Reena placed the I'm-excited-for-you smile on her face. "What can I help you with? I thought your mom and Lalita were coming as well."

"I asked them not to come," Anu said. "I don't want to do this."

"You don't want to get married?"

Anu smiled sweetly. "Of course I want to get married—I love Milan." She looked down at her hands. "I don't want the whole big fat Indian wedding thing." She looked from her hands to Reena. "Ms. Pandya. Seriously, the wedding is giving me panic attacks. I hate being the center of attention—I always have. This wedding is no different. I tried to talk to her, but she's all worried about insulting people. I just want to be married." The young woman shook her head, panic in her eyes; she had twisted her T-shirt into a knot. "Milan and I might just run away to Vegas—"

Reena took the woman's hands into her own. "I know it seems daunting. Let's not be rash. No need to be running off anywhere. You will be fine. I've dealt with nervous brides at every wedding. It's normal." She pulled out her I-hear-you smile. "You'll be fine." Followed by the suck-it-up smile.

"You really think so?"

"I do." Reena gave her the most reassuring smile she could.

"You know, when we were kids, we used to come here to see all the Christmas decorations, and it was soo beautiful." Anu shrugged her shoulders at the memory, a huge smile coming across her face. "Not to mention, Asha Gupta was going to be married here, wasn't she? Until her fiancé cheated. That must have been so awful for her."

Reena nodded and averted her eyes. "It was pretty horrible. Wait until you see the Diwali decorations. It's a first, but it will be amazing." Reena would be doing the decor herself, as she couldn't afford a decorator. Maybe she could get Sonny and Jai to help her. She just needed to keep this wedding at Lulu's.

"Even without all the hype, I've wanted to get married here my whole life. I just wanted it to be a smaller scale than what Mom has planned."

Reena phone buzzed. "Listen, Anu. I've got to take this. But you will be fine. We'll all be here to support you." She gave the young woman her I-believe-in-you smile and squeezed her hands.

Reena nodded to Kirti as she checked the incoming text from Sonny. Just a Bitmoji. They walked in the direction of the spa. "I'm glad you came," Reena said. "We're having some trouble with Ishani at the front desk."

"That's why I am here." Reena just now noticed that Kirti did not look her normal bubbly self. Her back was ramrod straight and her voice was cold. "Ishani has approached me. She's quitting."

Not surprising, considering she was having trouble with the job. Reena continued walking. "Do you have a replacement?"

"That is not the point, Ms. Pandya." Kirti had no trouble keeping the pace.

Reena was confused. "Then what is the point?"

Kirti stopped and looked at her, her dark eyes ablaze. She may not be biologically related to Akash, but they made the same face. "The point is that these women need to be *trained*. That's why they are here. Training implies that they are not familiar with how things are run. This is the third woman who has threatened to leave in three weeks."

"I thought they were desperate for work."

Kirti cleared her throat and stared at her. "Just because someone needs work, does not mean that they do not deserve to be treated with respect and kindness at the workplace." Kirti paused. "The women are leaving because of you."

"Me? That's ridiculous. This is a business. It needs to run."

"They need time to learn."

"They have time to learn. What I witnessed was incompetence."

"What you witnessed was part of a learning curve. What you saw was somebody doing a job that did not suit them." Kirti stood her ground. Reena was as impressed with her as she was irritated.

"You need them, as much as they need you, maybe more. They are not a means to an end. They are people. Who deserve the grace of a learning period." Kirti's eyes were fierce, but she gripped her tablet with white knuckles.

Reena stood. "What do you suggest? That I put up with incompetence?"

"No." Kirti paused and licked her lips. "We need to reassess the job positions."

"What difference does it make if they need to be trained?"

"Because everyone has innate strengths and weaknesses. If we know what they are, we can focus on that."

"I don't have time for that."

"But I do," Kirti said. "Let me make the assignments, instead of you."

This was what the young woman had proposed in the first place, but Reena had wanted to do the assignments herself. No one understood each job as well as she did. "That's…"

"You are a person interested in the ends, not the means. Let me take care of job assignments, and you'll get the results you need." Kirti was firm.

Reena studied the young woman. "Fine. We'll try it your way."

"One other thing. You might want to consider going to see Ishani and see if she will return."

Reena simply stared at the woman. "Why would I do that?"

Kirti typed into her phone, and a ding hit Reena's phone. "Her address," Kirti said. "In case you decide to go."

Reena didn't even glance at her phone.

Chapter Seventeen

Akash finally tired of working from the sofa in Reena's office or a chair in the outer office with James glaring at him every ten minutes, and insisted on office space at Lulu's. He had been ready to fight for it, but to his surprise, he no sooner asked than he was escorted to a small but workable space that afforded a window with a view of the city and the harbor, as well as a door.

There was not really room for Gemma, but she could do what was needed from home, and she was glad to do it. She FaceTimed him at least once a day.

"Your mom keeps calling the 'work' number." Gemma reported.

Akash stared at his phone.

"Mr. Gupta. Did you hear me?"

"Yes. I heard you. What did you tell her?"

"Nothing."

A knock at his door grabbed his attention. "Well, she's here. I'm not sure how she found me, but here she is."

"Who?" Gemma asked.

"My mom. Got to go." He ended the call. "Mom?"

His mother was casually but immaculately dressed in capri jeans and a loose blouse. She walked into his small office and sat down in the chair across from him. "I talked to your father."

"Okay." Akash threw up his arms. "So."

"He says you confronted him. About the divorce."

"Of course I did. I had to hear it from him as well." He plopped down in his chair. "I needed to hear his side."

"And?" his mother asked.

"And. And nothing. He has regrets. He denies nothing. He wishes you well." His irritation grew.

"But…?"

"But he still let me hate you my whole life." Akash burned with indignation.

"No. You did that on your own." His mother set her jaw.

"How can you defend him?" He leaned toward his mother.

"I'm not defending him. He was wrong. I left and made a happier life for myself. End of story." She smirked at him. "If your father is riddled with guilt, I can't say I'm sorry. But I have moved on."

Akash stared at her. "I was a kid. I didn't know what was going on. You left—"

"Yes. I left. I left your father, not you. Not your sisters." She looked him in the eye. "I tried to be there for you. You would not leave his side." She stood, apparently satisfied with her visit. "Yes, you were a child, confused, torn. I understand all that. You have not been a child for a very long time. There were no secrets. Had you asked, at any point in these last twenty plus years, the truth was yours." She took the few steps to his door. "I made your father promise me that much. That if you asked him why I left, he would give the truth."

He had.

"I never meant to abandon you, Akash. You're my son. I have been here for you all this time. I just didn't know how to make you see that. I hope you can forgive me for that one day," his mother finished.

Chapter Eighteen

It was the day before the big Patel Wedding. Toral Patel had five hundred guests for the whole day. Thank goodness for Amar Virani and Divya Shah. They were handling afternoon snacks and dinner and Sonny was doing morning snacks and lunch. Sangeeta was helping him, as the planner for this wedding was Lalita.

The decorations went up early in the morning, as did the mandap. Akash had wanted to come and see how things ran, so Reena had simply requested he dress like a guest, and stay out of her way.

While Lalita was not great at confrontation, she was incredibly organized, and preparations were going quite smoothly when Reena excused herself to change into her outfit. She wasn't a guest, but she liked dress-

ing up, and this was her first wedding as the owner—
kind of—of Lulu's.

She donned a simple cream-and-gold lehnga. Fancy
but not stealing the show from the actual guests.

At the allotted time, Toral and her husband, Amish,
approached the front door of the hotel from the inside.
The *taka-tum* of the dhol and accompanying music
blared from the street outside as the groom approached
with his baraat.

On Lalita's signal, the music was halted, and Toral
went to the door to greet the groom. Laughter reigned
king as the groom pulled the expected shenanigans with
his future mother-in-law, before he finally smashed the
clay pot indicating his intention to continue on with
the wedding. The Patels escorted him to the mandap
where the priest waited to start the ceremony.

Reena watched from a distance, careful to put her
I'm-so-happy-for-them smile on her face.

"That's your I'm-happy-for-them smile." Akash
came and stood next to her. Damn this man. He was
striking in a dark navy sherwani, light blue pants and
matching scarf. She had asked him to dress for the
wedding, so as to not draw attention to himself. Clearly
that was impossible.

She rolled her eyes. "Don't you have somewhere
to be?"

"I'm an observer today. Though your brother hooked
me up with the absolute best paratha I have ever had
with my chai." He made a horizontal cutting motion
with his hand to indicate finality. "Amazing."

"You're not supposed to eat," she chided, her brow furrowed. "The food is for the real guests."

Akash looked down at her with a small smile and a slight shake of his head while he handed her a familiar to-go mug. "Here, grumpy. Have some chai."

"I was looking for this!"

"I had James bring it down. Sonny put chai in it for you. Drink up. Maybe you'll be nicer to me."

She raised an eyebrow. "Not likely." She sipped her chai, and it did indeed improve her mood. "Thank you. For this." She gently bumped his shoulder. "I do feel better." He locked his gaze with hers and for just a moment, everything around them slipped away.

The dhol beat came closer and broke the moment. "Oh. Here they come." She nodded to the grand staircase that emptied into the lobby. The bridesmaids were slowly walking down to the hall.

"It's almost time for the bride," Reena said. Weddings excited her. She had no idea why. She had certainly not spent any time wondering about her own. But seeing all this, the energy of the celebration, the love in the air, it filled her with happiness.

"Look at you." Akash spoke softly near her ear. "You're downright giddy."

She shrugged one shoulder. "It's beautiful. The start of a young couple's life together."

Akash's eyes widened. "You are a romantic." It was an observation as much as it was an accusation.

Reena dropped her jaw in shock. "I am not."

"Yes, you are. Look at you, you are downright glowing." He shook his head at her, but then leaned in to her ear. "Truth. So am I. There's something about a wedding. The hope, the fresh start."

Reena turned to him, and then back to the approaching bridesmaids. "Too bad it isn't for me."

A young woman Reena recognized as Lalita's assistant exited an elevator and, walking as fast as she could, made a beeline for her. "Ms. Pandya. You have to come." The young woman was out of breath, and clearly trying to keep her composure.

"Come where?" Reena asked as she followed the young woman as fast as her heels would take her.

"The bridal suite."

Not good. "Why?"

"Just come."

Reena was vaguely aware of the fact that Akash had followed her close behind.

They took the elevator to the next floor above and hustled to the bridal suite. Lalita's assistant opened the door and Reena followed. Akash stood outside.

Reena could not believe what she was looking at. The bride was stunning, decked out in a red-and-white lehnga that sparkled in the sunlight coming in from the window. The red dupatta hung from the back of her head to the backs of her knees. She was currently sitting in a chair, shaking. Her mehndi-stained hands were clasped together, and her skin was pale. As Reena got closer, she could see sweat beading on her. Her breath was shallow, coming hard and fast. And there were tears in her eyes.

"Where's Lalita?" Reena asked.

"She's with bridesmaids. I'm supposed to stay with the bride."

"She's having a panic attack," Reena whispered.

"What do we do?" the young woman squeaked. She sounded like she might have a panic attack herself.

"Bring me a small damp washcloth." Reena knelt in front of the bride. "Anu?" She dabbed at Anu's forehead with the cloth.

Anu looked at her, almost not seeing. "How about some water?" She got Anu to drink some water.

"Hey." Reena smiled at her.

"Hey. I told you. I don't like crowds." Her voice shook, and her eyes brimmed with tears.

"There's just us three here." Reena smiled. "They can wait downstairs. You're the bride. Nothing happens without you."

Anu nodded. "My mom will be so mad."

"No. She'll be fine. Why don't we take a few minutes, then we can go down together, how about that?"

"I can't."

"Think about Milan. He's waiting for you at the other end."

She shook her head, tears flowing down her face. "No! I told you I couldn't do this. You didn't listen, Mom didn't listen and neither did Lalita. No one listened to me."

Reena's heart broke. Anu had indeed told her this would happen. She had dismissed it, focused only on the fact that the wedding would bring much needed income and publicity to Lulu's.

"I cannot leave this room." Tears dripped slowly

down her face, and Anu started shaking even more. "I cannot leave this room."

Reena nodded. She opened the door.

"Don't leave," Anu called out.

"I won't." She opened the door a crack, and thank goodness, Akash was still there. "I need you to go down and get the priest, the groom and both sets of parents. That's all. Not one more person."

"What's going on?"

"She's having a panic attack," Reena said. Akash nodded and left. Reena returned to Anu.

"I… I…told you." Anu was rocking back and forth a bit.

"You did. I did not listen. I'm so very sorry," Reena said gently, and she meant it. "Milan is coming up here so he can marry you."

Anu shot a glance at her. "He is?" A small smile broke through. "That's all we wanted."

A soft knock at the door. Reena answered it to find a highly irate Mrs. Patel. "What is the meaning of this?" She saw her daughter, and immediately knelt in front of her. "What has happened, Beta?"

"I'm sorry, Mom. I tried to tell you—I can't leave this room." Tears continued to flow down Anu's cheeks, her hands shaking.

"It's okay, Beta." Her father put his hand on her shoulder. "We're here."

Reena was riddled with guilt. Anu had come to her, told her this would happen. Reena had dismissed her concerns for her own selfish reasons.

Again.

"Ms. Pandya?" Mrs. Patel was talking to her.

"I'm sorry?"

"We were just asking if the couple could just get married in this room?"

"Uh, um—"

"Of course." Akash stepped in front of her. "That's why she sent for you all. This is where Anu seems to feel safe right now, and she stated her intention was to marry Mr. Shah." He nodded at Milan, Anu's fiancé. "As long as the maharaj is okay."

"I am fine." The priest looked at Akash. "If you wouldn't mind bringing that box of my things. My assistant is there. She will tell you."

"Of course." Akash looked at Reena as he started to leave. "You okay?" he whispered.

She shook her head. "No."

The rest of the event was a blur. Anu and Milan were married in a lovely and intimate ceremony in the bridal suite. The guests were fed and entertained, while Anu and her groom enjoyed a quiet day in the suite.

All Reena could focus on was the look on Anu's face. The true panic she had felt.

As the last guest left for their room, Reena found herself alone in the bar. The bartender brought her a dirty martini, but it sat untouched on the small table next to the sofa she had plopped herself into.

"Hey." Akash sat down next to her, motioning for the bartender to bring him a drink.

She turned her head to him and the tears fell. She could not have stopped them, even if she had wanted to.

"Oh. Hey." He wrapped his arm around her and let her cry. "What?"

"I knew."

"Knew what?"

"Anu. She came to me two days ago. Told me she couldn't handle being the center of attention, that she needed a way out of the huge wedding, but not the marriage. I ignored her. I needed this wedding to happen. I needed the guests, the whole thing. I just did not listen to her." Akash's arms were warm and comforting around her. She looked up at him. "My brother is right. I don't know who I am."

He cupped her face in his hands, wiping her tears with his thumbs. "You are Reena Pandya. But the question isn't who are you? The question is who do you want to be?"

She melted a bit into his hands. Sometimes it was just too hard to even keep her head up. "I don't want to be the person who causes young women to break down at their weddings."

"That's a start."

He was so close. He smelled so good. And it was very nice to have someone to lean on every-so-often. If she moved a few inches closer, she could place her lips on his and kiss him. As if he read her mind, he pulled back, dropping his hands from her face. "Come on. Get some sleep. I'll come get you at 7 a.m."

"What for?"

"Trust me. Just meet me out front. Wear shorts and a hat." He side-eyed her. "Top is optional."

Chapter Nineteen

Akash showed up with two to-go cups of chai and a picnic lunch packed by Sonny. Reena understood the assignment. He'd seen Reena in a business suit. He'd met Reena in a glitzy gown. He'd just seen Reena in Indian clothes. Nothing beat Reena decked out in shorts, T-shirt, sneakers and baseball cap and sunglasses, with her ponytail stuck out the back of the hat.

Well, except Reena wearing nothing.

She got in the car, her I'm-tolerating-this-not-knowing-stuff-for-a-few-more-minutes face fully on. He pointed to her chai and was rewarded with a genuine smile as she took her first sip.

"Where are we going?"

"We are going sailing," he told her.

"You sail?" She looked amused and impressed.

He nodded. "It's one of the things my dad and I would do when my sisters went to my mom's. He taught me to sail." He paused. "I guess it was his way of making up for messing everything up. Though I had no idea at the time. When we first went, I wanted to go on the big boat."

"Big boat?"

"He has a gigantic yacht, too. Full crew, etc. But he took me sailing. I didn't know it at the time, but the sailing is more fun." Akash grinned at her.

"Why are you taking me?"

"You seemed like you were having an existential crisis." He picked up his mug and sipped his chai. "I find that the water, sailing, helps with that. Plus, my mom told me to grow up the other day, so I need to go sailing and I hate going alone."

Reena smirked. "Did she?"

He nodded.

"We are quite the pair." She shook her head.

Except that they weren't really.

The drive to Annapolis was forty minutes, but the time flew as they conversed about the hotel and their parents and everything in between. Even the silences were comfortable.

When they arrived, he outfitted Reena in a life vest and they both got in the small sailboat. "So here are the basics." He went over the terminology and gave her some instruction. "Just in case a second pair of hands is needed," he told her.

When they were ready, they set sail. It was quiet and carefree. She was a quick study and understood the basics fairly fast. He took them out into the bay, and they floated for a bit.

"It's so beautiful out here." Reena said. "So quiet. You could really be alone with your thoughts out here." She made the life vest look good. "You know, figure out who I want to be."

"It's true. The water, the air. I don't know. Helps me focus," he said. "Not a bad gift from my father, considering he drove my mother away with his infidelity." Akash said.

"Maybe he wanted to make you feel better about missing your mom," Reena offered.

"He didn't want to tell me why she left. Because then I would have hated him and not her." Akash's answer was brusque.

"It's too bad you had to hate anyone," Reena said firmly.

Akash stared at her. "You wouldn't get it. Your parents are adorable."

"You're right. I really have no idea what it's like to have your parents divorce." She shrugged. "But I do know that hating someone is a choice."

He looked out into the bay, her words searing themselves into his brain. She was right. He had a choice. "Asha and Nila really missed her at home, in the beginning. Her visits were sporadic because he didn't really allow it early on. I suppose he was dealing with his own anger or shame." Akash said.

"You took care of them."

"I was the oldest. Don't get me wrong—there was plenty of staff, so I wasn't cooking, etc. But I read them stories at night, helped with homework. It helped me, to help them. You know?"

She nodded. "Sonny used to take care of me and Jai when our parents worked late. Although they managed to come home for dinner, I think they went back to work after dinner. But we did have that time with them." She paused, staring out into the water. "They were building Lulu's and I knew it. And I was so proud of them. I was happy with Sonny taking care of us – I didn't really know much different. And I knew even then that I wanted to be part of that. Part of building something from nothing, to continue what they had worked so hard for. It was...like a calling."

She stood and came over to sit next to him. She sat on the edge, just as a huge wave came and rocked the boat, knocking her overboard into the water. No sooner did she go over than Akash jumped in, trying to get her. The water was cold, but he hardly noticed as he was singularly focused on getting to Reena. A hollow pit formed as he looked around and couldn't see her. "Nonononono." He went under the water to try and see her.

Nothing. He came back up for air and glimpsed her hat bobbing a few feet away. He swam to it and found her there. He reached her and grabbed her arm. Relief flooded him.

"What are you doing?" She sounded downright irritated as she turned to face him.

"I'm helping you get out of the water." What did she think he was doing?

"You're saving me?" Her eyebrows shot up.

"Well. Yes."

"I think I lost my sunglasses."

He pointed to her hat.

She reached up and felt them there with her free hand, and rolled her eyes. "Great. Um…you can let go of my arm."

"Are you sure?"

She shook her head at him as he let go of her arm, and swam to the boat, easily lifting herself into it. He followed her close behind. The sun was warm and welcome after having been in the cold water. Reena was shivering a bit. He reached into a nearby bin and pulled out a few towels for them.

"Swim team." She smirked at him as she took the towel. "All four years of high school."

"I had no idea," Akash said, wrapping the towel around himself, and wrapping a second towel around Reena.

"Clearly." She eyed him as he covered her with the extra towel. "You have a real savior complex, don't you?"

"Well, I don't know about all that."

"I do. You are constantly 'saving' the people you care about. Your sisters. Nila came out to you first, because she knew you'd be there for her— to save her from anyone who didn't accept her. You saved Asha from, well, me. And you have tried to save me more than once." Reena watched him. "And not just from the bay."

Akash remained silent. It was just what he did.

"Is that what you think your worth is? Saving people? Helping people? Like if you don't save them, they won't love you?" There was no judgement in her words or her tone. She was simply asking a question or making a realization. Either way, she wasn't making light of him. She was a safe place for him.

"That's entirely too deep," he said, but she had touched a nerve.

"Doesn't mean it's wrong." She came close and sat next to him, taking his hand in hers. "You do not have to save people for them to love you. People will love you for who you are."

"That's just it, isn't it." He sighed. "I don't know who I am if I'm not saving people."

"Well then I guess we're both going to have to figure out who we are," Reena answered.

Chapter Twenty

Reena showered and dried her hair, a real smile on her face, as memories of her sailing afternoon with Akash popped into her mind. She should go to her office and get some work done, it certainly wasn't going to do itself, but she had something to do that was well overdue.

The incident with Anu had made it clear to her who she did not want to be. That would have to be a start. The day was surprisingly warm and pleasant for October in Maryland, so she walked the few blocks to Asha Gupta's building.

She pressed the call button. "Hello?" Asha Gupta's bubbly voice answered.

"Hey, uh, Asha. It's me. Reena. Can I come up? Just for a minute?" Reena asked. She waited for what seemed like an eternity while Asha decided what to do. Reena was about to leave when she heard the buzz. She grabbed the door before Asha changed her mind. She quickly stepped into the elevator for the penthouse before she lost her courage and changed her mind.

Reena stepped off the elevator in the penthouse, to find Nila and Kirti waiting in front of it. Asha stood behind her sisters.

"Come in," she said, jutting her chin at her sisters to move out of the way.

"Thanks for letting me up." Reena glanced at Kirti. Had she told her sisters she caught their brother outside Reena's room in the middle of the night some weeks ago?

"What can I do for you?" Asha asked. She remained standing.

"I just wanted to apologize to you." Reena lifted her chin and looked Asha in the eye. She could read nothing on the woman's face. "I...uh...knew about Rahul's infidelity, but I erased the video evidence because I didn't want you to cancel your wedding. I needed the wedding—your wedding—to help me bring in business, because I was on the verge of losing my hotel."

"You were going to let me marry a cheater, to save your business?" Asha's eyes widened in anger.

"Well, I wasn't going to let you marry him. I would have told you by the day before."

Asha stared at her in complete disbelief for so long, Reena was about to leave.

"So. Wait. You were willing to let me go through the whole week of celebration knowing that I would not be married in the end?"

Reena nodded.

"You were going to let me—and my friends and family—put on mehndi? Have a grah shanti puja, along with the pithi—all of it?"

Reena nodded again. It sounded horrible when she said it like that, but of course, Reena hadn't been thinking about anyone but herself.

"Oh, you are a piece of work." Asha shook her head at her.

"You're right. I am truly sorry. There is no excuse for what I did. For what it's worth, I'm going to do better." Silence again. "Thanks for hearing me out." Reena turned to go.

"Why come to me now? It's been like two months," Asha asked.

Reena turned back to her. "It seems….I had a lot of thinking to do. About what's really important in life." She paused and swept her gaze over the three women. "I thought I was some kind of amazing businessperson, but the reality is, that while I am a good businessperson, I sometimes lose my humanity along the way."

"I mean, it's terrible what you did and really not justifiable, but you're a great businessperson." Kirti piped up.

Reena nodded at her. Poor thing, her faith was likely misplaced. "Anyway. For whatever it's worth, I'm sorry."

"Or maybe you're apologizing because you're sleeping with our brother," Asha said.

Reena flicked her gaze to Kirti.

"I'm sorry. I am a terrible secret keeper." She had told.

"No. I'm apologizing because I mean it. Because I see how hurtful I was. As far as your brother, that was just a…fluke. Never going to happen again."

"Damn straight that's not happening again," Asha said. "He had a girlfriend for a while and he was really happy. Not sure what happened, but she's the one he should be with, not you." Asha leaned toward her. "I know you have to work with him. But outside of that, stay away from him."

Right. Got it.

Chapter Twenty-One

Monday came faster than was necessary. His birthday approached in less than a month, as did the JFL retreat and the Shah wedding in November. He ran into Kirti on the elevator.

"Hi. Any chance you have time for lunch today?" he asked her. "With me?"

"You want to have lunch with me?" Her eyes bugged out as they walked to his office.

He shrugged. "I do. Apparently, I need to grow up."

"Sure. I'll have lunch with you." Kirti's eyes lit up. "Who told you to grow up?"

"Mom."

"Yeah. She does that kind of thing." She chuckled.

They reached his small office. Reena knocked on his door with two mugs of chai. "Sonny delivered a thermos today. Rainy Mondays are the worst—he knows how to fix them," she said. She was fresh and gorgeous in a navy blue suit today. "Just a thanks for the sailing. It was a lot of fun."

"Of course." Akash's gaze lingered on her.

"Um… I need to get ready for morning huddle." Kirti passed her gaze between them. "See you for lunch, Akash. I'll just wait in your office, Ms. Pandya." She left.

"You're having lunch with your stepsister?" Reena whispered, as if they were conspiring.

"Yes." Akash widened his eyes as Reena watched him with amusement. "What, she's my sister, and I've been an ass to her. I'm doing the olive branch thing."

"Proud of you, for whatever that's worth." She gave him that pure Reena smile he loved so much. "Your mom would be happy to hear it as well."

Akash felt quite a bit lighter. Clearly, her opinion was worth quite a bit. But something was going on with her. He studied Reena's face. It was a futile activity. Reena never revealed what was going on inside. "Thank you. Is there anything else?"

"Why?"

"I don't know. But you have your I-have-something-to-ask-you smile."

Reena flushed, and it looked amazing on her. "To return the favor of taking me sailing, you are welcome to join me at the Pandya family dinner this Sunday. If you can stand the company, the food will be amazing."

"Sounds great." Why was he agreeing? He needed to stay away from her.

Chapter Twenty-Two

Reena sipped her chai at her desk. "James—was there any fallout from the weekend? How pissed are the Patels?"

"Not pissed at all. They are in fact grateful." James answered with a huge smile on his face.

"What?" Reena nearly spit out her chai.

"Yes. Apparently, having the ceremony in the bridal suite was a huge hit. The bride was happy, and therefore her parents were happy, and of course the groom. The guests enjoyed the food and live band. So, all in all, a success," James told her.

"The event was a success." Reena, however, had not been.

"Yes. We have interest from the two cousins—they are getting ready to book an engagement party and a wedding. Another family from the groom's side would like to book a Sweet Sixteen," James reported. "Their planners will be in touch." He glanced at his screen. "Looks like Sangeeta for all three."

"That's good news. Sangeeta really knows what she's doing. And fabulous, getting the events." But Reena wasn't feeling it. She had hurt that bride; she had hurt Asha. She didn't want to be that person. Apologizing to Asha had only been the first step in deciding who she wanted to be.

"Ms. Pandya? Did you hear me?" Kirti was watching her curiously.

"No. Kirti, I'm sorry. Please repeat."

"I was just saying that one of the employees has just reported some kind of leak. In the main ballroom."

Reena sat up straight. "What? James. Call—"

"I'm on it." He paused. "Maintenance will meet you down there in five. And I have alerted Mr. Gupta as well."

Reena hustled downstairs as quickly as her heels would carry her. Kirti was right behind her.

"What do we have, Mr. Cole?" Reena asked as she ran in.

"Well, right now, we have a leak in the main ballroom. And you can call me Jerry. You're all grown up now." He walked over to show her. "See?" He pressed his shoe into the carpet; water came up.

"I can hear the *but* in your voice—I've known you my whole life, Mr. Cole." Jerry Cole had been with her family since the beginning. He was in his fifties, stood a head taller than her with a bit of gray in his

blond hair. She used to follow him around as a teenager, fascinated with how everything worked and was
fixed. There wasn't a better head of maintenance in
Baltimore. But Reena could never call the man anything but Mr. Cole.

"But." He grinned at her. "You paid attention when I
taught you this. You know the ballrooms are attached.
So, water here, means—"

"Water everywhere." The Shah wedding was barely
four weeks away. Not to mention the JFL retreat. Her
mind raced. They were a boutique hotel. These were
the only ballrooms. There were conference spaces, but
no one wanted to get married in a conference room.

"The good news is it seems to be only a leak right
now." Mr. Cole told her.

"But how did it get to be so much water, if we just
found out about it?"

"Oh no. I told Mrs. Pandya about it when we first
found it."

"My mom? When was that?" Reena's heart started
to race. Her mother had known about this leak?

Mr. Cole looked at his notes. "February."

"February? Why didn't she do anything about it
then?" That didn't make any sense to her.

"We did. We did a patch. I said it wouldn't hold—
we needed to get a plumber in here to look at the pip-
ing." Mr. Cole looked around.

"What did the plumber say?" Reena asked when he
did not offer the information.

"We never called one. Mrs. Pandya said I worry too
much," Mr. Cole said quietly.

Did she? Reena started to fume. "Let's call a plumber now."

"Um...yeah." Mr. Cole looked away, suddenly unable to meet her eye.

"What? Just tell me." Reena pressed her lips together as if that would help her weather whatever Mr. Cole was about to tell her.

"Well, no one wants to come here. Word on the street is that Lulu's can't pay. I'm sorry, Reena. I thought your mom told you."

"No. She didn't tell me anything." Shame added to the heat in her body. "Well, we can pay our bills now," she managed through gritted teeth, as heat rose to her face. Would she never be free of her debt to Akash? "We have a Shop-Vac somewhere, don't we?"

Akash had started his morning quite successfully, as he was finally able to get some time to work on things that needed to be addressed with AG. He got an email from Charlotte at JFL confirming the date of the JFL retreat. It was the same weekend as the Shah wedding in November, but they could handle two events.

A text came through from James, just as he added it to Lulu's calendar. Leak in ballroom.

Akash hopped up and met Reena and his sister downstairs. He heard Reena assure Mr. Cole that they could in fact pay their bills.

Now.

He could only imagine her level of embarrassment to learn that Lulu's was known for being unable to pay their operating costs.

"I know a guy." Akash called out from the doorway. He tapped his phone and put it to his ear.

Reena turned to the sound of his voice. Kirti stood beside her, taking in the room.

Akash spoke into his phone for a moment, before ending the call. His step sloshed a little when he walked in to stand beside her and looked around. "My guys will be here in a couple hours. In the meantime," he looked at Jerry, "let's get all the Shop-Vacs we can find."

"Who is your guy?" asked Reena.

"Elijah Stevens. He has his own plumbing company. The company is new, but Elijah has been in the business a long time, and he does excellent work."

"How do you know him?"

Akash evaded her eyes. "Through work." He wasn't ready to tell her or anyone what his real work was.

He felt Kirti's eyes on him.

Mr. Cole's team brought up a couple small Shop-Vacs. Akash took off his jacket and rolled up his shirt sleeves to help suck up the water.

"Ah. Mr. Gupta. That is not necessary. We can handle it," Mr. Cole said.

"Just wanted to be useful."

"Suit yourself." The older man shrugged. "We could always use the help."

Reena had on her I'm-pissed-but-I'm-hiding-it-behind-my-lipstick face. "I have meetings scheduled. You all good here?"

Akash looked at Mr. Cole and they both knew. Reena was going to see her mother. He nodded at her.

"Do what you have to." She marched out, a woman on a mission. Akash might have felt bad for her mother, except that he was team Reena in this situation.

Akash helped out with the Shop-Vacs, until Elijah arrived an hour later. Elijah Stevens was some years older than him, and a few inches taller, but not new to the business. He was as reliable as they came. Akash explained the situation to Elijah, and in no time, his team was working alongside Mr. Cole's team to get to the source of the leak.

Elijah figured out the problem within the hour.

"I'll go tell Reena," Akash said. He texted her and found that she was still in the building. He went upstairs and knocked on her door. She was speed typing. "Hey. I thought you were going to your mom's."

She looked up from the laptop. "I never said that."

"True, but you were so mad—"

"I wanted the whole story before I went over there. I assume that's why you're here? To tell me the whole story?" She paused in her typing.

Akash walked in and stood in front of her desk, loathe to tell her. "I'm sorry. It's a burst pipe."

She pressed her mouth into a line. "How long?"

"Hard to say yet—they have to look at it, assess it and then—"

"We need new carpet, new drywall. I don't suppose you have contacts for that, given that you seem to have contacts."

"In fact, I do," he said.

"Contact them." Her voice was clipped. "Please. We need this done before the Shah wedding in three weeks. I need to run an errand." She grabbed her bag and brushed past him.

"Now, you're going to your mom."

"Damn straight."

Chapter Twenty-Three

Reena needed answers. It was close to noon when she was finally able to leave her office with all the information. She checked in with James and then made her way to her parents' house. They lived in a single-family home in the Roland Park area just on the outskirts of Baltimore. Close enough to work, but not in the downtown area.

Ten-year-old Reena sat on the plush sofa in her mom's office at Lulu's, crying softly. Her mother ended her call and then turned her attention to Reena.

Jaya Pandya was barely five feet tall, and hardly one hundred pounds soaking wet, and she was a force to be reckoned with. She was beautiful in the classic way, and she wore power suits to work. Reena and her brothers did not fear their father the way they did their mother.

She sat down next to Reena on the sofa, wiping away her tears. "What has happened, beta?"

Reena sniffled. "I didn't win the election. Bobby is the fifth-grade class president."

"Did you work hard?" her mother asked, one eyebrow raised.

Reena nodded.

"Did you give it everything you had?" She lifted Reena's chin with one finger so she had to look her mother in the eye.

"I think so." Young Reena nodded.

Her mother took Reena's face in her hands, gently, like it was something precious. "This is where other mothers would tell their children that so long as they worked hard and gave it their best, that's all that mattered. But I am not other mothers—you are not other children. Reena, you are a girl and you are brown. You will have to fight twice as hard to get half as much in this world. There is no room for failure in our lives. You must work hard, and you must do your best and you must win, every time." She had used her thumbs to wipe away Reena's tears. She had kissed her on the forehead and hugged her. When her mother pulled back, they both stood.

"I'm sorry to say, no ice cream today. When you win the election, we celebrate. Understand?"

Reena understood. Only winners reaped rewards. Second place got nothing.

* * *

When Reena arrived at her childhood home, the house was quiet. Only her mother's car was in the garage. Reena entered, removed her shoes and turned on the light in the kitchen. Some of her fondest memories were in this kitchen. Family meals after her parents had returned from a long day at the office. Or maybe they came home for dinner and then went back to work. She couldn't recall. She did remember that Sonny cooked and then the five of them would sit at this table and catch up on their day, while they enjoyed his delicious meal. Those were the best times.

The aroma of oil and spices lingered in the air; someone must have cooked. It was the scent of home, and Reena allowed herself to find comfort in it for a moment, before she went to confront her mother. She pushed aside those memories and feelings. She wasn't here for a stroll down memory lane. She was here for answers.

Reena went up the steep steps, past her old bedroom and on up to the spacious master bedroom. Her mother was in complete vacation-packing-organizational mode. The inexperienced eye would register mayhem, but it was, in reality, organized chaos.

Today, Reena was seething. "Mom."

"Oh hi, Beti. I didn't see you there." Her mother was petite and took great pride in her appearance. So even on a day when most people would simply don old leggings and an oversize T-shirt, Jaya Pandya donned designer moto leggings and a gorgeous loose-fitting, possibly silk, blouse.

"When did you find out about the leak in the ball-room?" Might as well get right to it. No point in for-mality here.

Her mother set her mouth and stood. "Which leak?"

"Are there more than one?" Reena felt panic rising.

"Not that I know of. If you're talking about that small drip in the large ballroom—"

"It is now a pipe that has burst because it was ne-glected. Carpets need to be replaced. We need new drywall, which will have to be painted, new window dressings…" Reena's voice was reaching pitches only dogs could hear.

"Oh. I had no idea." Her mother was irritatingly calm, seemingly unconcerned.

"Mr. Cole said that he told you about it in February."

"Of course. Yes. I remember. We never told you?" She went back to her folding.

"Obviously. I just found out because the leak be-came a small flood in my hotel!" How could her mother maintain her calm?

"Akash Gupta's hotel, isn't it?" The disappointment was loud and clear.

"It's *my* hotel," Reena continued from between clenched teeth. "And I'm hosting a wedding in a few weeks."

"Fifty-one percent, am I right? It's his." Her moth-er's tone was even, but disappointment dripped off every word. "If that young influencer had not been told of her fiancé's indiscretions, the wedding festivi-ties could have continued. Then you could have told her the night before. No one is harmed. The hotel gets business. Too bad you told her."

Reena stared at her. That had been her exact plan. But after Anu, after talking to Sonny, Reena knew she had been misguided. People would've gotten hurt.

"Sonny told her." Reena shook her head. He was braver than her.

"He was always soft hearted. Too bad, that wedding would have let you keep the hotel."

"I still have forty-nine percent." She sounded lame, even to herself.

Her mother raised an eyebrow at her. "I'm sure Jerry called a plumber, cleaned up all the water. So renovate." She shrugged. "You have been bugging us to do that for ages. *Akash Gupta's* money will help with that."

"Our regular plumbers wouldn't come, because apparently, Lulu's has become known for not being able to pay." She was shouting now. "It was humiliating!" Her mother kept folding clothes, as if she were over-reacting. She wasn't. "Not to mention, Akash Gupta's money is for operating expenses and loan payment. Not renovation."

"Semantics. Renovation is operating expense. You know that."

She did. She just didn't want to use Akash's money for renovation. "The point is why am I just now finding out about this? You should have told me when it was just a leak."

"You weren't here." Her mother continued folding clothes as if they were planning a menu.

"Of course I was."

"You were in Vegas. At that conference. You opted to stay an extra couple days," her mother said. "It was found then."

The blood from her head drained. She had been in Vegas. That's where she met Akash. She had extended her stay to have an extra day or so with him.

She had strayed from her goal for just a minute.

Gave in to happiness for a split second.

No one got ice cream for forty-nine percent.

Chapter Twenty-Four

When Akash met Kirti in the lobby for lunch, she was on the phone. She held up a finger to him and rolled her eyes.

He stepped away to give her privacy, but he could still hear her talking.

"Mom. Seriously. It's perfectly safe. I...yes. Of course... Mom. Okay fine bye. Love you."

Kirti turned back to him and he looked away as if he hadn't been listening.

"I know you heard."

He turned back to her. "Well, it's between you and Mom." He shrugged. "I didn't mean to..."

"Want to buy your little sister a drink?"

He feigned looking around. "Nila's not here."

Kirti hardened her face. "Fine." She spun around,

her curly hair following her, and started walking away, mumbling to herself. "I should have known better. What was I thinking…?"

Oh no. "Kirti." He started after her. "Kirti! Stop. Please."

She whipped around. "What?" she snapped.

"I was joking. Honest. Bad joke. Too soon. I'm sorry." Akash smiled at her. "It's what brothers do."

"How would I know that?" she snarked at him.

"Touché. Come on. We're supposed to be having lunch and I'm buying. You can tell me all about what's going on between you and Mom."

"I still want that drink."

"It's noon." He looked at his phone.

"I thought you fancy types had martinis or whatever at lunch."

"We do not live in the fifties, but sure, we can have a drink at lunch." He nodded at her. "Any place in particular you usually go?"

"I usually just hit the trucks outside," she said. "It's what I can afford."

"Always good! But if you walk with me, there's a place we can eat and drink."

Kirti sighed. "Sounds lovely."

They walked to a small bistro a few blocks away. Kirti ordered a glass of white wine, and he did the same. She ordered the burger, and he ordered the ahi tuna salad, to which she raised an eyebrow.

"It's healthier," he said.

They clinked glasses when the wine arrived, and sipped. He might have thought having lunch with his stepsister would be awkward, but he was surprisingly at ease. Kirti seemed to be as well.

"Mom does not want me to move out of the house." Kirti shook her head. "Like I'm still a child."

Akash stared at her. "What do you mean?"

"I mean I'm staying on-site for this internship so I can be around for whatever might happen—and so I can live somewhere other than with my parents. She's just afraid something awful will happen to me. I got into The University of Pennsylvania and she wouldn't let me go."

"She's trying to keep you safe."

"Oh, you're going to take her side—" Kirti narrowed her eyes.

"No. I'm just trying to understand her motivations."

Kirti pursued her lips at him. "Fine. She won't let me do anything. I want to move to Baltimore when I graduate. Maybe go to grad school, maybe work. But she insists it's not safe. Told me to move in with Asha and Nila."

"That might be fun for all of you." Akash tried to ignore the pang of jealousy he felt.

"It would be great. But, that's not the point. I want to live on my own. Make my way. Have my own space, you know?"

Akash nodded. "More than you could possibly even know."

"What do you mean?"

"I mean that everyone wants to make their own way, their own mark in the world."

"You mean you." She half-smiled.

"'The Force is strong with you,' young padawan," Akash quoted.

"And with you," she answered.

Akash grinned widely, impressed. "You like *Star Wars*."

She shrugged. "Duh."

"Your sisters don't." Or Reena. He'd found a *Star Wars* movie on the TV during their time in Vegas. She had rolled her eyes at him. She had definitely found a way to distract him from the movie, however. He smiled to himself.

"What's that smile?" Kirti raised an eyebrow at him.

He cleared his throat. "Nothing."

"Uh-huh." Their food arrived. "You were saying you want to make your own mark in the world."

He tucked into his salad as she bit into her burger. "I've only told this to one other person."

"Told what?"

"I'm leaving Gupta Equity. I have my own company, AG, but my dad thinks it's just a satellite company for his company. But it's not. It's mine. I want to be separate from my dad, as a company. I'm tired of the wheeling and dealing. I want to use my money for good."

"Wow. What kind of good?" She dug into her burger.

He munched on his salad, debating whether or not to tell her. No one else knew. There was really no reason not to tell her, or anyone else. Except that he hadn't told his dad. "What's on that burger?"

"Avocado, onions, spinach and some spicy sauce." She smirked at him. "It's amazing. Want a bite?" She held it out to him.

He reached for it, and she pulled it back. "What kind of good?"

"That is wrong. Holding a burger hostage like that."

She rolled her eyes again and held it out to him. He took it from her and took a bite. "Mmmm. This place makes the best burgers."

"Too bad you got salad." She held her hand out and he handed it back. "What kind of good?"

"The kind of good that pays for single moms to get jobs and have day care." He mumbled over a piece wasabi tuna.

She dropped her burger into her plate. "You? You put your own money into Lulu's?"

"Shhh." He looked around. "Not like all my own money, per se. It's a group. We pool our money and invest in things that have potential. When Reena told me about your program, I told the other investors, and they were on board." He glanced at her. "But yeah. It's mostly my money."

"Wait." Kirti stared into space. "I went to Reena like at least a month before you actually bought in. Did you two know each other—" Her eyes widened as she put two and two together. She pointed at him. "You two were together." She looked around the restaurant as if the answers were there. "And then she was going to let Asha marry that ass Rahul to save Lulu's and then you weren't together."

"Wait. How do you know about that?" Akash froze with his fork halfway to his mouth.

"She apologized," Kirti mumbled.

"Who did what?" He set down his fork and fixed Kirti in his gaze. "Start talking, little sister."

"Reena. Reena apologized to Asha." She shook her head at him. "But oooh." She dropped her burger. "Asha and Nila hate Reena. But they love the woman you were dating for a few months. Damn! Wait till they find out it was Reena."

Akash's stomach turned as he digested all this information. "When did this happen?"

"I don't know. Yesterday? After you went sailing."

"You can't say anything." Akash tried to stare her down.

Kirti shook her head. "Oh no, don't say that. I'm really bad at secret keeping."

Akash looked at her firmly. "You cannot say anything about any of this to anyone—got it?"

Kirti looked like she might be sick.

"Let's talk about getting you an apartment. You can't live in a hotel room all your life." Akash grinned at her.

"You're just changing the subject."

"Well, yes. But I am serious. What's your price range? I'll make some calls tomorrow, then we can go look."

"I don't have a price range. Unless I get a job." She picked up her burger again. "And there's still Mom."

Akash stared at her. "I'll talk to Mom."

"You would do that?"

He shrugged. "Of course."

"Or are you just doing this so I won't tell about you and Reena?"

"Suspicious much? One has nothing to do with the other. I helped Asha and Nila move out."

"I just need a job. I had a plan. Impress Reena Pandya. Get her to hire me." She sighed and tossed her napkin on the table. "But now she knows that I told Asha and Nila about you two hooking up—"

"You what?" Akash dropped his fork again.

"I told you—I'm really bad at secrets," Kirti repeated.

"Except the one about my dad being a cheater."

"Well. Yeah. But that was different. I wasn't supposed to know."

"You're not supposed to know any of this," Akash said, incredulous.

"Yet, here we are." Kirti widened her eyes. "I don't ask for secrets—they just come to me." She sighed. "Anyway, I'm not so sure Ms. Pandya will want to hire me…" She shrugged and then looked at him, a mischievous glint in her eye. "Unless maybe you sleep with her again and help me out."

Akash stared at her.

"Too soon?"

"Way. Way too soon." Akash narrowed his eyes at her and nodded.

Chapter Twenty-Five

Reena spent the rest of the week dealing with the burst pipe. Elijah's team had brought in a couple industrial-sized Shop-Vacs and sucked up the bulk of the water. But now they needed drywall people and carpet people, and thankfully, Akash seemed to have contacts in all these fields.

Every company that came by seemed to know him personally and was more than happy to do the work even though they'd heard that Lulu's had been in arrears. While Reena was grateful that she had contractors to do the work, she was also increasingly aware that none of this would be possible without the money Akash had put into the company.

It irked her and soothed her all at the same time.

By the time Sunday rolled around, Reena was tired

of takeout and reheated food. She wanted a home-cooked meal, and a couple hours in the bosom of her family. Even if that meant seeing her mother while she was still angry.

At four in the afternoon on Sunday, Reena left her office and knocked on Akash's door. He wasn't there. She texted him. Where are you? We have dinner in 30 minutes.

His response was immediate. I'm home, like normal people. I went to the gym.

Reena: Fine. I'll be there in 10.

Akash: No. I'll come to Lulu's. It'll be faster.

Reena: Whatever. Mom hates it when I'm late.

She waited in her car for Akash to arrive.

"Dinner at the Pandyas'. At your own risk." Reena lowered her sunglasses to look at him as he got in the car. He was casually dressed in jeans and a fitted T-shirt. She missed seeing him like this. Casual, relaxed.

He met her eyes, ran his gaze over her. "You're in a work suit."

"I came from work."

He glanced at her again. "Diamond studs go better with that outfit," he mumbled.

She flicked a glance at him. "I gave them back."

"I know." He was quiet for a moment.

She put the car in gear and headed for the highway.

"You gave back the diamond studs, but you kept my UMD T-shirt?" he asked, a smile in his voice.

She half-smiled. She loved the soft, worn-in feeling of that T-shirt. Besides, it still smelled like him. It was a sad commentary, maybe on her state of mind, but she preferred the old T-shirt to the earrings. "Priorities."

He shook his head at her and faced forward. "Hey! Whoa! Look out!" Akash grabbed the dash with his hand and turned to her like she was crazy.

Reena had learned to drive on the streets of Ahmadabad during summer vacations at their grandparents. Lights were suggestions, lanes were optional, honking was required. It was the epitome of "if you can make it there, you can make it anywhere." Sonny had learned to cook with Dadi, and Reena had gone driving with her grandfather. Every time she drove, she thought of Dada, and a smile filled her face. He would be proud of how she drove now. But, a little voice nagged at the back of her mind, would he be proud of how you acted in business?

She casually turned to Akash, all innocence, as she promptly cut off an SUV with her Civic. "What?" She couldn't help smiling at his pale face. "Do you get carsick?"

"Only when I'm the passenger in a death machine." His eyes were wide and he still had his hand on the dash.

"I've never even been in a fender bender," she announced proudly as she lay into her horn. "And I have never gotten a ticket—for anything."

She turned to see Akash's eyes bug out. "If they're

going drive below the speed limit, they need to get out of the left lane."

"No kidding." He made a huge show of clutching his heart when she finally parked in front of her parents' house.

She laughed. "It's not that bad. Get in the house. Papa will get you a drink to calm your nerves." She waited while he got out of the car, and then she pouted her lips. "Aw. Was that too much for you?" she teased as she placed her hand over his heart. She gasped when she felt the thudding of his heart in rapid fire. "You really were nervous."

"What did I say?" Though he spoke quietly and placed his other hand over hers as he met her eyes.

The closeness was too much for her; as much as she enjoyed it, she knew she couldn't allow herself to go there again. She pulled her hand free and stepped away from him. "Let's get you that drink."

They entered the mayhem that was the Pandya family dinner. Football season had started, which meant the game was on for sure. Her father's sister, Mira Foi was decked out in a purple football jersey and was already shouting at the TV along with Jai and her cousins. Her mother and father were putting finishing touches on the multitude of foods they had made; Sonny was trying to taste everything, and either learning, or making improvements.

Sonny stopped midtaste when she came in, Akash behind her. "Reena's here," he announced to the crowd.

Jai turned toward her and waved.

Her father walked toward them. Her mother nodded

as she opened the oven. "Beti!" her father said, enveloping her in a huge hug. "Mr. Gupta." He offered out his hand to Akash. "Good to see you again."

"Please call me Akash." he said as he shook her father's hand and gave him the bottle of wine he'd brought. "Sorry we're late, we were—"

"Working," the crowd stated in unison.

"Well, she was working," Akash clarified. "I was at the gym."

"Hah!" Jai called without turning away from the game. "Reena Ben got a normal one."

"Reena Ben didn't get anything, squirt. We work together," Reena said as she walked over to hug her little brother and lightly smack the back of his head, all while avoiding looking at Akash.

"You never bring James over," he accused.

"I have so brought him over. You and the Pandya cousin gang scared him off," Reena insisted.

Jai shrugged, waving her off, and turned his full attention to the game.

Meanwhile, her father had opened the bottle of red Akash had brought and was going on about its merits. "This may be one of my new favorites. Jaya, you must try this." He took a glass to her mother.

"Good to see you, Akash." Sonny came to greet them. He hugged his sister. "What are you drinking?"

"Sauvignon blanc for me." She looked at Akash.

"Beer for me," Akash answered.

Sonny nodded and left to get drinks. "Where's Sangeeta?" Reena asked.

"She has a client meeting," he called out as he poured her wine.

"Mom." Reena walked over to her mother and gave her a huge hug that was returned with loads of affection. They might be irritated with one another; in fact, Reena was quite irritated with her mother, but they were family. And at Sunday dinner, they tried to put all that aside.

The evening was spent drinking and eating and telling stories. Reena had missed these gatherings; they fed her soul. As she had promised Akash, the food was second to none. She glanced at Akash, who was sitting at the opposite end of the table. He was engrossed in conversation with Sonny and one of their cousins, looking every bit like he belonged here. That was the beauty of her family; everyone was welcome. It was kind of what made them the perfect hoteliers. They were the consummate hosts.

Reena called it a night a few hours later, saying she had to work. It was true, but her whole family tried to lure her away from the office.

"Come, Akash, there must be something to get her out of the office," a cousin had asked.

He shook his head, but the pressure was relentless. "I took her sailing last week," he finally said.

The room went nearly pin-drop silent. Only the sound of TV was heard. "You took her sailing?" Sonny asked.

"And she went—willingly?" Jai added.

"Yes." Akash furrowed his brow. "What's the big deal?"

"The big deal is that Reena doesn't do anything except work for the hotel," Sonny answered. "You accomplished what we have all been trying to accomplish for as long as we can remember."

Akash looked at her, a grin of victory at his lips. She gave a one-armed shrug, as if it were all inconsequential.

"So, wait." Jai spoke up. "You know how to sail? And you have a sailboat?"

"Yes. And yes," Akash answered.

"Are you open to taking Reena's brothers?"

"Of course. Say the time," Akash suggested.

"Next weekend," Jai said.

"I can do that." Sonny nodded his head.

"Perfect. It's a date." Akash actually looked quite happy. He turned to her and nodded. "As long as Reena's game."

Reena caught her mother's eye, the slightly raised eyebrow, the gentle pucker of the lips. The last time she had indulged in herself, the leak had gone unresolved. She couldn't afford for that to happen again. "I'll be fine. You all can go."

Chapter Twenty-Six

"You don't have to take them sailing—it's fine," Reena told him as she drove them back. *Drive* was a loose word for what she was doing. Though, if he looked carefully, she was *traversing* traffic very well.

"Are you afraid to let your brothers go sailing with me?" Akash was already looking forward to it.

"No. I'm afraid for you. Sonny and Jai seem nice, but—I don't know." She side smiled.

"What do you mean?"

"They think we're dating. They'll grill you." She lay on the horn again.

"But we're not dating, so it doesn't matter."

"Fine." Reena wove through three cars as if she were making a simple right turn. "I just know my family cornered you into it. They do that a lot, by the way. I should have warned you."

"I love sailing. And I don't go as much as I'd like," he said watching her. "I don't have brothers to do these kinds of things with." She snapped her head to him. "Not that they're my brothers. But they're guys. Not my sisters." He quickly backtracked.

Her jaw was clenched. The only sign on her that indicated she might have a concern about something. "You're welcome to join."

She stared ahead. "I'd love to, but I'm sure I'll have a ton of work to do. Wedding and retreat coming up, the burst pipe."

"One day, Reena. Just plan for it. You had so much fun last time."

She remained silent. Akash had not seen this side of her before. The side that was torn between something she clearly wanted to do, and something she felt she should do.

"Does this have anything to do with your mom?" he hazarded to ask.

"No. Of course not." She cut off another SUV.

"I saw how she looked at you."

"I'm not a child—I make my own decisions. Not my mom."

"Glad to hear it. Have James block off your schedule then."

She squirmed in the seat, then seeming to not be able to squash it, she smiled. "It's not that."

"Then what is it?"

"The last time I gave in to what I wanted, the leak happened."

"You lost me."

"The leak in the ballroom? Mr. Cole told my mom about it while I was in Vegas." She flushed. "With you. Those extra days we took?"

"They were amazing." Akash could not help the warm feeling he had whenever he thought about that time. Which was more and more these days.

"Yes, they were." She agreed, nearly sighing. "But by the time I got home, my mom had 'dealt' with the leak. And now it's a burst pipe. If I had been here back then, we wouldn't be dealing with this now." She paused. "There's no ice cream for second place."

"What?"

"Just something my mom used to tell me." She shrugged as if it didn't matter, but Akash had the distinct feeling that it really did. "She was preparing me for the world. I'm a brown woman. I have to work twice as hard to get half as much. So, I just need to always be on top of my game."

"That seems harsh," Akash said.

"Maybe. But it's true. She was just trying to set me up for success." Reena shrugged.

"She's tough."

"No tougher than your father."

Akash thought about it a while. "True."

"I thought you were going off on your own, leaving Gupta Equity," Reena said as they sat in traffic.

"You remember that?" He turned to her.

She shrugged. "I remember a lot of things, Akash."

The way she said his name, just then, so intimate. He melted. He immediately started to think of ways to get her to say his name again. "I have already put the move into play."

She snapped her head to him. "You kept that quiet. What happened? What did he say?"

"He doesn't know yet."

"But you're supposed to become a partner in like a few weeks."

"Yes. Wow. You really do remember."

"Have you forgotten anything?"

He didn't answer. The truth was he hadn't forgotten one thing.

"Why haven't you told him?"

"My family isn't like yours."

"Meaning?"

"Meaning you just had it out with your mom about the leak not being properly addressed, but tonight, you were downright cozy with her."

Reena chuckled. "She's my mom. We don't always agree, in fact we disagree quite a bit. She's tough and overbearing and demanding, but I love her, and she loves me." Reena shrugged. "The rest, we figure out. It's what most people call being in a family." She looked at him. "What are you afraid is going to happen if you tell him?"

"That he'll think I'm abandoning him."

"Isn't that why you never went to your mom's? Because you didn't want to leave him alone?"

"Yes."

"Akash. Stop living your life for other people. You need to do you. *Tell him.*"

She'd said his name again. What was it about his name on her lips? "Fine. Let's make a deal." Traffic opened up and they were moving again. Reena's attention was on the road.

"What kind of deal?" she asked.

"You need to enjoy life. The whole 'second place doesn't get ice cream' is BS. If you keep putting off your life, your enjoyment, until you reach a certain goal, you'll never reap the rewards of your hard work. Live a little." He paused. "You come sailing with me and your brothers next weekend and I'll—"

"Tell your dad you're leaving Gupta Equity?" she finished, her face glowing. "Deal."

"Seriously?"

"Heck yes. I get to go sailing!" She laughed.

"Great." He smiled at her and looked out the window just as she quickly pulled up to the car in front of them. Akash was sure she was going to hit it, and he braced his hands on the dash, preparing for the impending crash. She braked hard and his seat belt locked, but the sound of metal on metal did not come. He opened his eyes to see the other car a mere inch from their car.

"Damn it. We're stuck in traffic again," she said as if they hadn't nearly just lost their lives. She glanced at him. "See? You survived that. Talking to your dad should be a piece of cake."

He closed his eyes and rested his head back on the seat.

"Why are you so sweaty?" he heard her ask. "Want me to turn up the AC?"

Chapter Twenty-Seven

Reena sauntered in Monday morning at eight, feeling refreshed and eager to get to work. She'd had a fabulous run and had snagged chai from her brother. She paused as she took in Akash leaning against James's desk. He was in a crewneck T-shirt, dark jeans and a jacket. The jeans fit just perfectly, as did the T-shirt over his muscles. Casual *hot* elegance. She caught herself as warm gushy feelings came over her. She stood straight and fixed her face into neutral. Can't be having any of that.

"Good morning," she said brightly. She handed Akash the extra chai she had gotten him from Sonny. "Courtesy of my brother. Something about surviving a car ride with me."

Akash smiled and it was a breathtaking thing. When

he smiled, his eyes lit up, transforming him from serious businessman to hot sexy businessman. He was always clean-shaven in a field of men who had embraced the casual scruff. Heat rushed up to her face. She looked away. "What's first today, James?"

James glanced at his monitor, a knowing little smirk on his face. "Well, as I was telling Mr. Gupta," he flicked his gaze to him, "your first meeting is with the Shahs."

"What does that have to do with Mr. Gupta?"

"Nothing," Akash said. "James just informed me that Mrs. Shah is probably the most demanding mother of the bride that you have ever dealt with."

James turned to Akash. "Sudha Shah actually gives our Reena a run for her money."

"Does she now?" Akash asked. "This I must see."

Reena sighed and closed her eyes. "Nothing a little chai can't handle."

"They are waiting for you in the lobby," James said.

A mild spark of panic hit Reena. "You kept them away from the ballroom, right?"

"Janki is on it. She's a top notch hotel mamanger. They won't get anywhere near the ballroom." James smiled and cut his eyes to Akash. "See what I mean?"

Reena sipped her chai and rolled her eyes. "Do you think it's wise to let Mrs. Shah know that the ballrooms are wet? Three weeks before her daughter's wedding?"

James glanced at the time. "You might want to hurry before she gets bored."

Reena's eyes widened and she pivoted back to where

she had come from. She felt Akash behind her, heard his small chuckle. "Are you amused?" She asked.

"Actually, yes. Yes, I am."

She entered the elevator and turned around as he followed behind her. "Well, I hope you are still amused if it turns out that Mrs. Shah has found the wet ballroom. According to Mr. Cole, it should be ready to go with only one day to spare before the Shah-Jones extravaganza gets going."

"Extravaganza?"

"I'm not even exaggerating. Andrew Jones got a permit to close off the block so he can ride in on a horse." Reena rolled her eyes.

"Seriously? People still do that?"

"If they have money, they do. To each his own, I say. But Mrs. Shah? She would strike terror in even Mrs. Patel from last week," Reena said.

"I can't wait to meet them."

"Save yourself. Don't do it."

"I survived two car rides with you." He held up his chai. "I can handle one middle-aged wealthy auntie."

It was Reena's turn to smirk. "Okay." She sipped her chai as the elevator doors opened. She stepped out and nearly bumped into Kirti.

"Hey, Ms. Pandya. Sorry. I was just on my way to tell you that we can give you a tour of the day care facility at 10 a.m. today."

"That'll be fine. I'll head over after this meeting."

Kirti's face lit up. "Awesome. I can't wait for you to see."

Akash walked beside Reena, sipping his chai.

"Are you sure you want to help me handle this auntie?" She turned to find him raking his gaze over her bare legs. Her body tingled as if he had actually touched her. Nope. No time for that.

"Hm?" His gaze was still on her legs.

She tiled her head and caught his eye and narrowed her eyes at him. "I'm up here. You paying attention to me?"

"Of course."

She stopped and stared him down.

"I'm sorry I was distracted for a moment. It won't happen again. You were saying?" Akash made a show of looking her in the eye.

"What distracted you?" She raised an eyebrow at him.

"I…uh." He cleared his throat. "I don't want to say."

She furrowed her brow at him as if he were a child. "Uh-huh." She shook her head at him. "Whatever. I need to get Mrs. Shah before she gets bored and starts wandering."

She turned and started walking.

"I've never seen you in a skirt at work before," he blurted out.

She stopped and slowly turned back to him.

"I'm sorry. You have beautiful legs… I mean you're a beautiful woman… I mean, that's not workplace appropriate—never mind—can we just go see this auntie?" Smooth and suave Akash Gupta was blabbering. About her legs.

Reena took two steps closer to him, so she was close enough to just graze his body with hers. She looked up at him and spoke softly. "You have seen much more than my legs. Get over it and let's move on."

She stepped back quickly because now she had given him images of …the rest of her. Not what needed to happen before this meeting.

Akash cleared his throat and nodded.

"Ahh! There you are, Reena!" A petite and slightly round middle-aged Indian woman called to Reena from across the lobby. She waved and walked over quite quickly, considering the height of the heels she was wearing. She clutched a Chanel bag.

Reena glanced at him and walked out to meet her. "Mrs. Shah!" Reena greeted the woman like she was a long-lost friend.

"Reena, beti. Call me Auntie. Mrs. Shah is so formal." She laughed. She glanced behind Reena and stopped, her smile widening. "And who do we have here?"

"Mrs.—Auntie, this is Akash Gupta. He…uh… works with the hotel now."

"A very fine addition indeed." Mrs. Shah did not even attempt to hide her pleasure at seeing Akash. Nor did she bother to lower her voice. "Beti, he's not wearing a ring. Snap him up quickly before some other, less deserving woman does."

Reena hoped the flush on her face was not as evident as the flush on Akash's face.

"It is very nice to meet you, Auntie," Akash said amiably.

"So polite, too." She giggled like a young girl.

"Auntie," Reena rolled her eyes behind her back. "What can I do for you?"

"Oh." Mrs. Shah seemed to snap back to herself. "I just wanted to be sure we were on track for everything. Rooms, gift bags, decor, etc."

"Auntie, we have discussed this. All those questions are for Sangeeta. That's why you pay her," Reena told her.

"I have talked to her. She said everything was set."

"Then it is." Reena nodded and chatted with Mrs. Shah as if there were nothing she would rather be doing, when in actuality there was a pile of work on her desk.

"I know. I just," she looked around, "I just want everything to be perfect for Dina's wedding."

"It will be—I promise," Reena assured her. "Sangeeta is a fabulous planner. Lulu's can't wait to show off, but most of all, come what may, by the end of the evening, your daughter will be married to the love of her life."

"Of course you're right," Mrs. Shah agreed. "Mind if I walk past the ballroom?" She started to walk ahead.

Before Reena could open her mouth, Akash was at Mrs. Shah's side. "Actually, Auntie. I'm the new owner here, and I'd love to hear all the plans you have for this wedding, so we can incorporate the ideas into a new program Reena and I were just discussing. It's a program for our more *discerning* patrons. The bar is open and I hear that the chai has improved. Care to join me?"

He glanced at Reena and she nodded thanks to him,

apparently so relieved that she didn't care he was making things up as he went along.

"That would be lovely," Mrs. Shah said, hooking her arm with his. "Reena, beti. Thank you."

"Anytime." She wiggled her fingers at Akash as he led Mrs. Shah to the bar.

Chapter Twenty-Eight

Reena cut to the ballroom to check progress. The carpet people Akash had called were starting to pull the carpet up and the old drywall was already down.

"Mr. Stevens." Reena recognized Akash's plumber friend. "How are we progressing?"

"It's coming along. I know you have a tight time schedule, but it can only dry so fast, you know what I mean?"

Reena nodded. She did.

"Don't worry, ma'am," Elijah said. "Akash has never failed anyone. And he's not about to start now."

"How exactly do you know Akash?" Reena asked.

"Years ago, the company I worked for merged with another. I lost my job. Had two kids in high school, headed for Ivy League schools, and I was out of a job. Akash found me a job with this plumbing company—it wasn't actually my field, but it was a business—work that I needed, with a bonus that I could grow it. I learned everything I needed to know, and just last year, when the owner retired, I bought him out. Akash Gupta is a good man. He helped me when I really needed it. I know it was his father's company that brokered the merger, but Akash," Elijah shook his head, "is not his old man."

Reena smiled at the plumber. "No. He most certainly is not." Akash would have taken it as a personal responsibility to make sure this man had work and his family was taken care of. Her phone dinged a ten-minute reminder of her meeting with Kirti at the day care. "Thank you." She nodded and looked around. Lulu's was in good hands.

Kirti and Akash were already waiting for her in the employee wing where the day care was located, chatting amiably, laughing even. Kirti dressed as she always did. Black pants, black blazer, white button-down, ballet flats. Today, she had left her hair down, the tight curls bouncing as she talked.

Reena smiled to herself. Akash had another sister. He was almost a different man when he was happy. She hadn't seen him this happy since…well, there was no reason to go down that road right now. "Good morning." She nodded at them both. They both stopped talking abruptly when she greeted them.

"Mrs. Shah is happy, I assume?" She turned to Akash.

"She is."

"Thank you for that." She smiled at him.

Reena looked from Akash's face to Kirti. "What am I looking at here?"

"Oh. Yes." Kirti tapped her tablet, before grinning widely at Reena and Akash. "I want you to see the day-care facility we set up." She walked and they followed.

Reena glanced at Akash and smirked. He furrowed his brow in question. She mouthed the word *sister* and smiled at him with a thumbs-up. He shrugged and rolled his eyes. Then he made eye contact with her and mouthed the words *thank you*.

They followed Kirti down the hall and stopped in front of one of the adjoining rooms. Kirti stopped dramatically before opening the door. "Now we made changes to the interior, so it's kid-friendly. The women who aren't on shift are able to work here, but we also have women who work the day care as part of the program. Their own children are involved as well. The younger and older children are separated—"

"Kirti," Reena said gently. "Let's see it."

"Oh. Of course." Kirti opened the door, and it was almost another world.

These rooms were adjoining suites, so they were on the larger side. The one they entered was set up for the younger children, very much like a preschool. Bright primary colors advertised the numbers and the alphabet. One corner of the room was set up with a rug and pillows surrounding a rocking chair and a small set of shelves with books. Another area was set up with paints and two tiny easels. There was a board game section, and a science section and a—

"Is that a goldfish tank, Kirti?"

"Oh, um…yeah. We read that having a pet was good for the children. A fish seemed the least…intrusive."

Reena nodded and beamed at Kirti. The space was incredible. "This is amazing. Well done."

"Very nice." Akash's voice betrayed his pride, which somehow added joy to Reena's heart.

They walked in and looked around. Reena took in every detail. There was a gate put up between the two suites, and the other room was for the older children who came after school. That room had tables for doing homework, as well as some things similar to what the younger children had but more age appropriate.

"Depending on what kind of help we get, we are thinking to have a few field trips, such as a visit to the aquarium, which is just down the road," Kirti added. "All of these children have hope for better than they have because all of their moms are working. They live in the poorest neighborhoods, food deserts, where they are witnesses to violence. It's hard for their mothers to find jobs that allow them to also ensure their children's safety. Working here, they can do that," Kirti said proudly. "You made this possible."

"You are truly incredible, Kirti," Reena said, her heart swelling. "And it wasn't me. It was you who made this possible. I just needed capable staff."

A young woman, maybe a year or two older than Kirti, approached Reena. The woman's thin face shone with happiness as she extended her hand. "Hi, Ms. Pandya, I'm Mary."

"Nice to meet you, Mary." Reena shook her hand.

"I work with Housekeeping. I must thank you for opening this up to us. I am so excited to be working here, knowing that my child is well cared for by these other women. If it weren't for you and Lulu's—" Tears brimmed in her blue eyes. "Well, let's just say, this is exactly what I needed. What we all need."

"Well, I'm happy to have you. To be honest, you're all helping me. I have had staffing issues for a time now, and I am so excited to have you on board. This hotel is my family legacy and I want it to thrive again." Tears burned at her own eyes. "And now thanks to you, I think it might."

Her mind wandered to Ishani, who Reena had been so abrupt with, she hadn't even heard her out. She turned back to Kirti. "You have great potential for anything you want to do. Don't apologize for speaking truth to power."

But one should apologize for using power incorrectly. "I have to go." She needed to fix this. And she needed to fix this now.

"Where are you going?" Akash asked.

"I'm going to right a wrong. Or at least apologize," Reena said as she left. She felt Akash following behind her.

"Reena Pandya is going to apologize? *This*," he said, "I have to see."

"You can stay here. Hold down the fort." She walked fast.

"The fort will be fine for—how long will we be gone?"

"I don't know. Couple hours." Now that she had decided to do this, it could not happen fast enough. She tapped her phone.

"What are you doing?"

"Calling an Uber."

"I'll drive," Akash said as he headed for the employee parking lot. "Meet me out front in ten minutes."

"Yeah. Okay." Her mind was spinning and her heart was starting to ache as it started to sink in exactly how unfair she had been to Ishani.

Ten minutes later, she was in the front seat of his Honda. She giggled. "You drive a Honda?"

"Yeah." He shrugged as glanced in the rear view. "What of it?"

She shrugged. "I guess I had you pegged as a Lexus guy."

He grinned, sheepish. "I just sold the Lexus." He chuckled and Reena laughed.

"Why?"

He frowned and occupied himself with his side mirror. "Just didn't really use it. No sense in having an expensive car like that simply sit in the garage. So, I got this instead."

"But you had a Lexus—I was right?" she insisted.

"Yes," he capitulated. "You were right."

"Ha!" she said as she settled into her seat. "I guess we never went anywhere in a car, so I had no idea."

"I mean it's no Civic." He chuckled.

"Hey. It's great for parking in the city."

"You have special parking at the hotel," Akash countered.

She waved him off. "Details. It was the first thing

I bought on my own. I wanted something practical, not flashy."

So typical Reena, everything should have a function. "So, where are we going?"

"I put the address in your nav."

"I'm aware. But *where are we going*?" He side-eyed her, and she squirmed in her seat.

"I…made a mistake. I treated one of the trainees terribly. I was only thinking of myself and what I felt needed to be done. Seeing the day care, meeting Mary, made me realize just how Kirti's program was supposed to work. It's not all about my hotel. In fact, it's barely even about Lulu's. It's about those women being able to provide for themselves and their children." She looked down at her hands. Her heart ached with regret over treating Ishani so harshly. "She may not want to come back and work for me. But she deserves an apology." Reena looked at him, then out the window.

Thankfully, Akash said nothing. A few minutes later, he pulled up in front of an older apartment building. They got out and Reena checked her phone. "Unit four twenty-six."

They walked up to the fourth floor. As they neared that floor, Reena inhaled the tantalizing aroma of garam masala, garlic and onion. The thick scent of frying oil hung in the air. Reena knocked. A few clicks as the door was unlocked, and Reena found herself facing Ishani. Her hair was in a bun, and she had on apron over jeans and a cotton salwar kameeze top. The wonderful food smells were coming from her apartment.

Upon seeing Reena, Ishani folded her arms across her chest, and hardened her eyes.

Reena heard Akash's stomach rumble, just as hers did the same. "Ms. Sharma," Reena said.

"Ms. Pandya. What are you doing here?" Ishani peeked around Reena and Akash as if there was something she was missing.

"I came to apologize," Reena said.

Ishani narrowed her eyes at Reena but did not move. "Who is this?" She nodded at Akash. She had a slight Indian accent.

"This is Akash Gupta. He owns a portion of Lulu's."

Ishani grinned at him. "Ah-ha. So *you* made her come down here?" She bobbled her head.

"Not at all. I just drove," Akash said smoothly. "Do you think anyone can convince Reena Pandya to do something she does not want to?"

Ishani nodded her agreement to this statement and stepped aside, inviting them both in. Reena and Akash entered her small apartment and found every surface covered with food. There were fluffy idli, puffed up poori, large square khaman sprinkled with chili and cilantro, various shaks, and of course, samosa and pakora.

"Everything smells wonderful." Akash inhaled, proving his point. "And such a fabulous variety."

"Mom!" A voice called from the kitchen. "How's this?"

A little boy, no more than eight, came out to the family room area, holding what looked to Reena like a perfectly filled samosa. He was small and thin, his hair rumpled. Ishani walked over to him and examined his work. "Getting better." She spoke gently. "Can't have this hole, though—all the oil will go inside."

The boy nodded and retreated to the kitchen to fix it. He glanced at Reena and Akash, before attending his business.

"Is that your son?" Reena asked.

Ishani stared at her.

"Yes okay." Reena looked her in the eye. "I came here, to apologize to you for treating you unfairly. I was out of line, singularly focused and I did not show you the respect or understanding that I should have. I am very sorry." She paused. Ishani simply watched her, not even blinking. "On further thought, it has now occurred to me that your computer skills might be just fine, but you get flustered dealing with belligerent people. And the man you were helping was belligerent. I should have told him off for being so rude. Instead, I found fault with you and that was wrong."

Silence filled the spice-scented air. After a moment, Reena spoke again. "Well. Don't let me keep you from your cooking." She nudged Akash. Ishani did not owe her anything. "We can see ourselves out." She turned to go.

"I cook for people because it's the only way I can earn money and still be here for my son. We have no family and his father passed away three years ago."

"I am very sorry for your loss." Reena nodded.

Ishani said, "Sit. Eat."

"Oh no—" Reena started.

"That would be fabulous!" Akash said. "I'm starving. She," he poked his thumb at her, "didn't even let me eat before we came. Not to mention, everything smells fabulous."

Reena glared at him.

"What? It's rude not to eat."

Ishani smiled at Akash. "Of course. Sit, sit." She cleared an area for them to sit at her dining table. "Sometimes girlfriends can be like that." She jutted her chin at Reena.

"Oh no. I'm not his girlfriend." Reena spoke up immediately.

Ishani looked to Akash, the question on her face. He nodded. "She's right."

Ishani smiled at him. "Maybe that's better for you."

Akash chuckled. "Maybe."

Reena spoke between closed teeth. "Ha-ha."

"Ah. Here we are." Ishani returned with two plates heaping with samples of everything they could see as well as whatever she had on the stove. "You might have to share." She smirked at them.

Akash grinned at her. Reena was nearly intoxicated from the fabulous aromas and did not care in that moment what Ishani thought of their relationship. They started to eat. Every bite was better than the last.

"Taste the idli," Reena commanded him, holding a piece out to him with her fingers. "Seriously. So soft and fluffy." His hand was already holding a piece of rotli wrapped around a mouthsized amount of shak, so he opened his mouth. She fed him the small piece of idli, his lips grazing her fingers. He groaned.

"You're not kidding. I've never had such a light idli."

He held up the pind he had made. "This bhinda nu shaak is out of this world. And her rotli, super thin." He held up a bite for her and she ate it from his fingers. Spices came alive in her mouth, and her whole body tingled. Okay, the tingling was probably from having Akash's fingers touch her lips.

She nodded. "Did you try the paratha?"

He scanned his plate. "I didn't get it."

"Oh my god." She ripped off a small piece of the pan-fried flat bread and scooped up some homemade mango pickle held it in front of his mouth. He didn't even hesitate. He took the bite and smiled. "Mmm. So good."

They spent the next twenty minutes in a culinary heaven, tasting the food, feeding each other. Everything was fabulous.

Ishani watched them with a furrow in her brow. "Are you sure you are not a couple?"

"We're sure," they chorused.

Reena looked around at all the food, then met Akash's eye. She turned back to Ishani. She and Akash spoke at the same time. "We need a chef."

"I am not a chef," Ishani said.

"Are you sure?" Reena gestured around at the food.

"I learned from my mother and her mother." Ishani shrugged.

"People pay you to cook for them," Akash observed.

"Yes. I am a good cook. But I am not a chef." Ishani crossed her arms in front of her.

"I don't care how you learned, as long as you're good," Reena said. "If you're interested. You have amazing talent, Ishani. I—we would be honored if you came to run the restaurant at Lulu's."

"I don't know business," Ishani said, but Reena could tell she was thinking about it.

"Not a problem." Akash spoke up. "We will ask Kirti to find someone who knows business to run it. You just need to cook."

Reena put her hands together. "Please. I can get my brother to walk you through how to utilize a commercial kitchen. Then I'll get Kirti to find a few people to help you out."

Ishani's eyebrows raised at that.

"You'd be the boss of the kitchen. They would do your chopping, etc.," Reena said.

"Dishes?"

"Yes. We will get you someone to wash dishes," Reena agreed.

"How much?" Ishani pursed her lips as if debating, but Reena saw the interest in her eyes.

Akash gave her the number they had reserved for the chef.

At the number, Ishani let her guard down. Her eyes widened and she stepped closer to them. "Seriously?" She looked at Reena.

Reena nodded, her mouth full of idli again.

"What about Veer?" She nodded at her son.

"He'd be at the day care, of course," Akash answered as Reena was still chewing.

"Even in the evening when I cook dinner?" Ishani raised an eyebrow.

"Of course," Reena answered.

"Then. Okay. I will do it." She smiled at Reena. "He is good for you." She glanced at Akash.

"We're not together," Reena insisted.

"Well, maybe you should be," Ishani stated, smiling at them both.

At this, Reena felt heat rise to her face. She did not look at him. "When can you start?"

"One week. I have a few obligations I need to take care of."

"That would be great," Reena answered. "I'll talk to Sonny. And thank you very much."

Ishani smiled and nodded. On an impulse, Reena hugged her. Ishani was surprised, but she hugged Reena back.

Chapter Twenty-Nine

Akash peeked over at Reena as they drove back from Ishani's house. She had smile on her face, biting her bottom lip as if she was trying to rein in her excitement for what had just happened.

"You did a good thing. You should be proud," Akash said.

She flicked a gaze at him. "You think so?"

"I know so," he added.

"Even though I was the reason I had to apologize? I mean if I had been kinder to her to begin with, I wouldn't have had to apologize."

"The point is that you realized what you had done and tried to make it right," Akash told her.

"Well, I won't be making that mistake again."

"I do believe that is the point." He smirked at her. He was rewarded with a gentle punch in the arm.

"Ow."

"Faker. Wait, where are we going? We just passed the turn for Lulu's." She twisted in her seat to point to the turn he did not take.

"To a speakeasy for a drink. We need to celebrate."

"We need to celebrate the fact that I apologized? I mean I know I'm stubborn but come on—"

"We have a chef!" Akash stated. "Or did you forget the absolute best part of the whole day where we ate amazing food?"

"She really is an amazing cook." Reena settled back into her seat, the huge smile back on her face.

"Honestly, I've never had idli like that." Akash laughed. "Do not tell my mom."

"Or my brother. Though I believe Sonny would be impressed." Reena laughed along with him. It was a beautiful sound.

He parked and they had to walk a bit to get to the speakeasy. They entered through an indistinct side door and traveled back in time. The lighting was dim, only small mushroom-shaped lamps on each table. The main room was divided into initimate areas with sofas, loveseats and plush chairs. Alongside the walls were tables for two with curved love seats.

All of the sofas were full, even at one in the afternoon, so Akash led them to a small table along with two curved seats facing each other. It was as if they were in their own personal bubble. Reena ordered her standard extra dirty martini; Akash ordered his old-fashioned. He raised his glass to her. She raised hers and they clinked glasses. "To hiring a chef."

"To hiring a chef," Reena echoed. They sipped their drinks and set them down. "This place is amazing. I really feel like I'm hiding out, doing something illegal."

"That's the point." Akash watched her. She was relaxed, happy, enjoying the moment. She was beautiful.

"What?" She caught him looking at her.

He grinned at her over his drink. She never ceased to amaze him. Her ability to grow and learn and change was one of the things that had drawn him to her. "You're stunning."

She flushed. "We'll have none of that talk." But she smiled all the way out to her dimple. "The credit goes to Kirti. For bringing that program to me. She's incredible." She stared into her drink and then back at him. "Thanks for coming with me."

"We offered her a chef's salary, you know," Akash said as he sipped his old-fashioned. The drink was strong but went down smooth and easy. He relaxed into his chair, into Reena's company.

She smirked at him. "It's not my money."

He cocked an eyebrow at her. "I see how it is."

"She's going to work hard. She deserves it," Reena commented, smiling.

"I can't remember why I let you go," he said without thinking.

She stared at him a moment during which he found her unreadable. When she answered, her voice was not as hard as he would have expected, but different, wounded maybe somehow. "What makes you think you let me go, and I didn't just leave?"

He stared at her. Leave it to Reena to make him question everything. "Either way. Maybe I should have…fought harder."

She shrugged. "No guarantee it would have worked."

He laughed out loud. "So true. You're a lot of things, but easy is not one of them."

She narrowed her eyes at him. "You, however, are quite easy." She laid her hand on his and squeezed gently. The zing ricocheted throughout his body. Her hand, so much smaller than his, was warm and strong. He had missed her touch.

He met her eyes; she was watching him. Why had he let her go?

"Thanks for your help with Mrs. Shah today," she said.

He shrugged. "Can't have her walking into a damp ballroom, can we?"

"Absolutely not. But quick thinking on your part." She wiggled her eyebrows at him. "Though I'm sure you made her day."

Akash laughed as he waved off her comment. "I don't know about all that, but she's still having the wedding at Lulu's. Which, by the way, is the same weekend as the JFL retreat."

She nodded. "Not a problem. The retreat is smaller. We can convert a couple conference rooms for them while the wedding is going on, and we can use the outdoor space on the fourth floor for their evening event. Let's try to staff the spa for massage services by then. I'm really excited. The whole thing will give all the guests the idea that Lulu's is booming again." She squeezed his hand and moved in conspiratorially and she brought with her the scent of flowers and her fading perfume. He wanted to drown in it. "Great for future business."

"Of course." He nodded, but his attention had become fixed on her scent, proximity and her lips.

She paused and he caught her gaze flick to his mouth and his whole body heated. The instant way he responded to her was all at once wonderful and mortifying. If he leaned in just a few millimeters, his lips would touch hers, and it would be heaven. Their night together haunted him every day. As did the morning after.

It took every bit of self-control to not move closer to her, to not lean in and place his mouth on hers, where it clearly belonged. Instead, he removed his hand from under hers, instantly feeling the loss of her touch. He placed some bills on the table. "We should get back."

"Yes. Of course." Reena sat back, slightly flustered, but she recovered quickly, reaching into her wallet for some cash.

"Don't worry about it, Reena. My treat. We're celebrating the new chef." He forced himself to sound casual, nonchalant.

She smiled at him and put her wallet away. "That is very kind of you. Thank you." The formality was back. Gone was the relaxed Reena. Better this way.

He stood and they walked back to the car, making plans for the new restaurant, setting up a meeting with Kirti for the next day to get more staff. They put the speakeasy behind them and talked about business.

"We need a name for the restaurant. Something new." Akash said as they drove back to Lulu's.

"That's the hardest part for me." Reena laughed. "How about Joy?"

"Joy. I like that. Who would not want to eat at a place called Joy?"

"I was joking."

"It's still a great idea," Akash said.

"Let's say that Joy is our working name, until we think of something better."

Akash laughed and shook his head. "Whatever." This was nice. Spending time with Reena, working together, laughing. This was how he had imagined his life with her. "I do have a favor to ask."

"Uh-huh?" Reena looked over at him, instantly suspicious.

"Relax. It's just that I have a family wedding to go to, but I need a date."

"Why? Your family will be there."

"Because you know what happens when you show up at a wedding alone. And you're single."

Reena grinned. "Aunties."

"Yes. It's the wedding of a family friend. Someone my dad knows. Their son. So, we get to go to the jaan."

"What do I get out of it?" Reena asked, ever the businessperson.

"You get to scope out the new hotel in town."

"I'm listening," Reena said.

"The one that's more downtown. The Epic." Akash

raised an eyebrow. He could tell she was interested. Always great to check out the competition.

"Fine. When is it?"

"Next week."

He parked in the garage, and they entered the elevator together. They were in the elevator, alone. It brought back memories of their first time together. He smiled at the memory, and side glanced at Reena. She was looking straight in front of her, a small smile and a flush on her face. He'd bet anything she was thinking the same thing.

The doors opened to the lobby and he waited for her to exit before getting off behind her. "I'll go check the ballroom," he said.

She smiled thanks. "I need to go over those spreadsheets if I'm going sailing with you on Sunday."

He brightened at the thought of spending even more time with her. "Better get to it."

"Don't forget your end of the deal," she reminded him.

He waved her off as he walked in the direction of the ballroom.

"Hey, Nicole!" Nicole Thompson's company was in charge of the drywall and new carpet.

"Hey, Mr. Gupta. I was just getting ready to text you. I'm sorry but we have a problem." Nicole's voice was steady and serious. Nicole was a few years older than him, and her demeanor was normally serious. The current look on her face was serious, even for her.

"What's going on?" Akash asked, a tightening in the pit of his stomach.

"Mold." Nicole pressed her lips together.

The knot in Akash's stomach filled with acid as he stared at Nicole, waiting for more info.

"There's mold under the carpet and in the walls," Nicole told him.

Akash tapped a number in his phone. "How much?" he asked Nicole while the phone rang.

"Half the room. At least. We're still pulling up carpet in the smaller ballroom. But there's mold in there for sure." She shook her head.

Akash swallowed the expletives that came to mind. "Hey. Lorraine," he said to the woman who picked up the phone. "I need your help." Lorraine owned a company that handled mold remediation. If anyone knew how to take care of mold, it was Lorraine.

He handed the phone to Nicole so she could give Lorraine the details. Nicole ended the call and handed back his phone.

"She is sending a team over day after tomorrow to take a look." Nicole explained. "That should be enough time to get the rest of carpet up and peek behind the drywall."

Akash drew his gaze over the ballroom and sighed. "Let's just keep this between us until Lorraine gives me a timeline for remediation."

"Sure thing, Mr. Gupta."

Chapter Thirty

Reena sat down in front of her computer to finish up the dreaded spreadsheets. Not that she particularly dreaded them. In fact, the organization and simplicity of a spreadsheet was something she found reassuring. Something she and Sangeeta had in common. It was more that she had been enjoying her time with Akash, in a way she hadn't in a while. Truth was, she was enjoying him in a way she never had before. As a friend. Not that they hadn't been friends, but things had moved very quickly for them, and she wondered if they hadn't skipped through the "getting to know you part" too fast. She was looking forward to going sailing again. With him.

Reena hadn't missed how he had looked at her. In fact, she had enjoyed it. Maybe a bit too much. She could have sworn he was going to kiss her at the bar. She had certainly been considering kissing him, putting her lips where they loved to be. But that would have been to her detriment. She couldn't keep kissing him if she couldn't have him.

So then why was she going sailing with him on Sunday? That annoying little logical voice asked. That was different. Her brothers would be there, first of all. And he was right, she needed to get away from the office every now and then. Sonny had been telling her that for years, but she was finally feeling the need to do so.

So, sailing with Akash—and her brothers—was self-care, which would only help her reach her goal of owning Lulu's by her next birthday.

She felt good about her meeting with Ishani today. Bonus, they had found a chef for Lulu's.

She lost herself in the spreadsheets and then a few phone calls and had no sense of time passing until she was startled by a knock at her door.

"What's up, James?" She looked up to find Akash holding a pizza, and a bottle of wine. "Oh. It's you." She felt a smile fall across her face. Not to mention she was completely thrilled to see him.

"It's me." He sauntered in bringing the aroma of garlic and onion and tomato with him.

"Wow." She inhaled deeply. "That smells like—"

"Nina's?"

"Yes." She stood. "Is it? Did you go all the way to—"

"Well, they delivered," Akash confessed, coming into her office, and setting the pizza on the table next to the sofa. He found her wineglasses and twisted off the cap of the wine and poured. "And you need to eat."

Her stomach growled. "I was so engrossed, I lost track of time."

Akash grinned at her. "I remember."

She stared at him just then. But then quickly recovered. They sat down and clinked glasses and sipped before starting in on the pizza. "How's the ballroom coming?"

"Fine," Akash said, not quite meeting her eyes. "Carpet is still coming up. Drywall still coming down. Nicole's company can take care of all that."

"As long as it's ready for that Shah wedding. Mrs. Shah may be demanding, but she's also connected to a bunch of people. If she's happy, we're golden." Reena dug into the pizza. "This is my second favorite comfort food."

"Sonny's khichdi is your first." He looked at Reena. "But he didn't make it today." Akash shrugged. "So, I went with number two."

She paused in her eating to stare at him. How had he known all of this about her? "What's your favorite comfort food?" Reena asked him around a bite of the pizza. "You know, something that makes you feel better, feel…loved."

"I guess I would have to say my mom's mixed pakora," Akash answered, sipping the wine. "She used to make it for us on rainy days—it was my favorite. She'd make them fresh and hot, along with spicy cilantro chutney and tangy tamarind chutney."

"Garam-garam." Reena laughed.

"Yes!" Akash agreed enthusiastically. Then his enthusiasm faded. "But I haven't had that since I was a child."

"So, have you talked to your mom? Since, well, everything?" Reena asked.

Akash shook his head. "She came to see me, but it was…not great."

"Why?"

Akash shrugged. "I was so horrible to her all these years, and all that time, it was my dad who was the asshole. I don't know where to start." He downed his wine.

"How about with *I'm sorry*?" Reena suggested.

"Seems lame, like it's not enough."

Reena shrugged. "You won't know unless you try. She's your mom."

"Every family isn't like yours, Reena. We don't just hang out and get along, just because we're family. When we're hurt and angry, we're hurt and angry."

"It's the same for us. But we all always still love each other. My mom irritates the hell out of me, but she's my mom. And I love her." Reena shrugged again. "Don't you think, after being so awful to her all these years, you at least owe your mom an apology?"

Chapter Thirty-One

The next day, Akash tracked down his mother at Asha's house. Apparently, she felt better staying there, if Kirti was going to insist on staying at Lulu's. Akash had tossed and turned all night thinking about what Reena had said. He did feel like a terrible son having treated her like the villain all these years.

He had hurt her, and all she had done was take care of herself and love him.

The elevator doors opened, and Akash entered to a seemingly empty apartment. "Hello?" he shouted.

"Right here," his mother called as she walked out of the spare bedroom.

"Hi," he said, suddenly awkward with his own mother. "Mom."

"Akash." She stopped and stared at him. "I didn't

know you were coming. I would have made chai for you."

"That's okay." He moved to the kitchen. "Why don't I make chai for you?"

"You. Want to make chai. For me?" His mother looked astonished.

"Sure. Can't a son make chai for his mother?"

She shrugged. "Of course. You just never have."

He pulled out a pot and filled it halfway with water and set it on the stove to boil. "Well." He looked at his mother. "It does seem like the very least that I could do."

She sat down on a stool on the outside of the kitchen counter, facing him. "Is that so?"

He turned away from her to add the loose tea and masala to the water. Facing her was much harder than he had anticipated. No matter. He turned around. "Do you take sugar?"

"Just one spoon."

"Me, too." He smiled. "So Kirti wants to get her own place."

"How do you know?" His mother asked, a small smile playing at her mouth.

"She works at Lulu's. We had lunch." He shrugged like it was no big deal, even though it was.

"You had lunch? With Kirti?" She leaned toward him.

"That's what I said. Mom, she's twenty-two."

His mother shook her head with vigor. "It's too dangerous. She can live here with Asha and Nila."

"She can get a small place between here and my

place. I live—not too far from here. The three of us will check up on her. She is our sister."

"She's your sister now?"

Akash didn't look at his mother, instead, concentrating on the chai. "You know, my favorite food is your mixed pakora?" He changed the subject and turned so he was facing her again.

"Really? Kirti loves them, too." She shook her head and looked away. "Though that was probably because I made them all the time." She rested her gaze on him and he saw the years of pain he had caused her, and his heart broke.

"You made them all the time?"

"Yes." She nodded at him. "Time to add the milk."

He turned back to the stove and added the milk to the pot, along with the sugar, and lowered the heat so the pot simmered. He leaned with his back against the stove so he could watch the chai and still see his mother. "You made them all the time because it was my favorite." He wasn't sure if that realization made him feel better or worse.

Tears filled her eyes. "It was silly." Her words were thick with the effort of holding back her tears. "But... yes."

"Mom." He turned heat down on the chai and leaned across the counter to her. "Mom. You were right. About me. I never even bothered to find out why you left. I assumed it was me, so I cut you out of my life, the way I perceived you did to me." He placed his hand on hers. "I'm sorry. I cannot change the past. But I would like to be your son again, if that's okay with you."

She wiped away the tears that had fallen. "You never stopped being my son, beta. I want you to know, that even though we didn't see each other, you always had a mother. I do not require an apology, but it makes me happy that you want to share your life with me again. That you know that I am, and always have been, here for you." She put her hands on the sides of his face. "All I want is time with you. Like this. Having chai." She glanced behind him. "That is about to boil over."

He jumped away from her and to the stove, lifting the pot off the heat just before it all boiled over. He looked at his mother over his shoulder. "Saved."

She chuckled as she wiped her eyes. "You're welcome."

He laughed as he strained the chai into two mugs. "Well, Kirti is growing on me. She's very smart and tough and persistent." He handed one mug to his mother. "Just like her mother."

She turned her attention to the chai he had made. She swallowed and then sipped her chai. "Wow. Pretty good." She gave a half smile. "But mine is better."

He clasped his hand over his chest and feigned pain. "I'm still learning."

"Keep practicing." She laughed. "There is one more thing, Beta, a larger lesson."

"What's that?"

"I think you leave people before they can hurt you. It's protective. But understand, that in doing so, you could be sacrificing the one thing you really need."

Chapter Thirty-Two

Akash would be picking her up bright and early for sailing tomorrow morning, but Reena wanted to check the work schedule for the week. Although Kirti had been managing it well, they would have a chef in a week, so the schedule might need some shuffling around.

Kirti's idea of honing in on people's strengths and matching them with jobs that used them, or finding their weaknesses and working on them, was making for a happier work environment all around.

Even Reena was happier. She decided to attribute that to a smoother-running hotel, but the little voice that lived in her heart insisted that some of the credit go to the time she was spending with Akash. She was getting to know him in ways she hadn't when they were together. Their interactions had been so intense, something as banal as having a drink and pizza together was not something that had ever come up. But she had quite enjoyed having pizza and wine with him.

"Hey there." A knock at her open door pulled her away from the Tetris game that was the weekly schedule.

"Sangeeta. Hey. Come in. Just going over the schedule. What's up?" Reena asked.

Sangeeta came in, looking a little flustered.

Reena turned her monitor away and focused on Sangeeta. "What did my brother do now?"

Sangeeta flushed and shook her head. "Oh. No. He didn't—he's great." She paused. "It's my business."

"Your business?"

"Yes. I've never run my own business before. The gathering of clients, the actual planning and execution, I can do. I even have an employee."

"That's wonderful." Reena was genuinely happy for her. Sangeeta had an eye for detail, and a natural need to plan ahead, so she was in her ideal field.

"It's just the actual business part. Managing the income, employee salary, taxes, the schedule—it's all so overwhelming." Sangeeta's eyes widened. "I'm in over my head, and I didn't know where to go."

"Sonny couldn't help you?"

Sangeeta raised her eyebrows, her eyes filled with hope. "Sonny said you helped him get set up."

"You want me to help you get set up?" Reena was incredulous. But even as she asked the question, her mind flooded with ideas.

"Well, yes. I know you're super busy with—"

"No. I mean yes. Of course I'll help you." All thoughts of the dreaded weekly schedule out of her mind, Reena grabbed a blank piece of paper and started writing. "Here is what I do each week, in the hopes of a smooth week, but before that, you need to get these things set up." She looked up at Sangeeta. "Did you bring your computer?"

"Yes." Sangeeta smiled and pulled it from her bag.

"Perfect." Reena stood and walked over to her sofa, motioning for Sangeeta to follow. "Get comfortable."

Sangeeta sat down and opened her laptop.

Reena peered over her shoulder. "Show me what you have right now. We'll work with that, and then I'll show you what to do next."

"Right now?"

"Yes." Reena was eager to do this. Whose business was this, anyway? "James?" she called out.

"Yes, ma'am." He popped his head in.

"I'll be here working with Sangeeta. Mind ordering us delivery from that bowl place? And then you can go. Not sure how long we'll be here."

"You're sending me home early?" James furrowed his brow.

"Yes. If you don't mind ordering us dinner before you go?" Reena asked.

He stared at her a minute. "No of course not. I'm just—is everything okay?"

"Everything is fine, James. Don't act like I never sent you home early before." Reena had the urge to put her hand on her hip.

James shook his head at her. "Not in the four years I have worked for you. Not once."

Reena blanched. "Well, then it's well overdue."

"Thank you so much," James called from his desk.

Reena looked at Sangeeta. "Lesson number one. Let your staff go home early every so often."

Chapter Thirty-Three

When Akash picked up Reena bright and early Sunday morning, she appeared to be dragging a bit, stifling a yawn as she got in the front seat of the car. Sonny and Jai were already in the back and had insisted that Reena sit up front.

"Late night?" he teased. "Those work schedules will get you." He handed her a to-go cup of chai, which she immediately brought to her lips.

"I didn't even get to the work schedules. I was working with Sangeeta until close to midnight," Reena said as she sipped the chai. "Chai's good, but you're slipping, Bhaiya."

"Not my chai," Sonny called from the back.

Reena side-eyed Akash as he pulled back into the street. "You?"

Akash gave a one-armed shrug. "It's a work in progress. What were you doing?"

"She was teaching an up-and-coming entrepreneur," Sonny said.

Akash's turn to side-eye her.

"Sangeeta was struggling with the business part of running a business, so I gave her some tips." Reena shrugged like it was nothing, but her face glowed and her smile was telling.

"She texted me last night," her brother informed her. "It was really helpful, Reena. I tried to help her, but I kept forgetting things. I'm glad you went over things with her."

"It's the same thing I did for you."

"What about me?" piped up Jai.

"I'll do it for you, too." Reena turned to smile at her brothers.

"Weren't you teaching some of the new staff about personal finances the other day?" Akash asked.

"Well, they were asking—"

"I think you were very helpful to them, Reena." He paused and looked at her. "Something to think about."

They arrived at the dock in Annapolis and had the boat out in no time. All three siblings were interested in all aspects of sailing, so Akash gave them a crash course, and then helped them do different tasks.

"What is that boat? It's called *Asha-Nila*," asked Jai, pointing to a huge yacht parked some distance away.

"That is my father's yacht. He uses it for large business parties, usually," Akash answered, without really looking at it. He had never really understood why his father owned the thing when he used it maybe four or five times a year. Not to mention that he had named it for his sisters.

When Akash had asked about the name, his father had waved a dismissive hand and told him that no one put male names on a boat.

"Have you ever been on it?" Jai asked.

"Nope. He doesn't let anyone on it unless he's entertaining," Akash answered. He had never been invited to go to those parties.

"Hey, Jai," Reena called, "come, let me show you how to do this."

Jai turned to his sister and was immediately distracted away from the yacht. Reena lowered her sunglasses to look at Akash, concern flitting through her gaze. He pressed his lips together and gave a small shake of his head. He was fine. She replaced her sunglasses and turned her full attention to Jai.

Sonny pulled out snacks and Akash handed him a beer. "I don't know how you did it, Akash, but you got her out. And not out for a business dinner, but out on a sailboat. Twice."

"She's a workaholic, huh?" Another thing he hadn't really registered during their short time together. Things had been so new between them that all either of them did was go to work and spend time together. Other interests never came up.

"Well, she's focused. Our parents busted their butts to get Lulu's to where it is today. Reena has always had a special connection to Lulu's. Maintaining and having Lulu's progress, I think is Reena's way of honoring the sacrifices they made, of ensuring that their life's work wasn't for nothing, you know? So, when she goes to extremes, while it may not always be the right thing to do, Reena has blinders on and doesn't always see that. She is singularly focused."

Akash concentrated on Reena as she sat with Jai and watched the sail fill with wind. She laughed at something her younger brother said, the wind tossing around the few pieces of hair that escaped her ponytail. Sunglasses hid her hazel eyes, but the smile on her face was carefree as were her shoulders. Akash realized it had been rare that he ever saw her this way. She had always been professional and polished, the only exception being when she had been in his bed.

"Any guy who might want a chance with her would have to accept her dedication to Lulu's. It's in her DNA, in a way that it's not for me and Jai."

Akash whipped his gaze to Sonny. Reena's older brother had fixed an intense gaze on him. "My sister can take care of herself. But, if the man isn't careful, it may not end well for him."

Akash just stared at him. What did he know?

"Don't look so surprised. No one hangs with Reena just for the hell of it. She's not that fun." He shrugged.

"Is that so?" Akash asked, nodding toward a laughing Reena. "She looks like she's having fun right now."

Sonny smirked at Akash as he brought the bottle to his mouth. "That's exactly it." Sonny sipped his beer, the smirk now paired with amusement. "She's also never brought anyone to family dinner."

After an exciting day sailing together. They piled back into the car.

"Hey, Akash. Mind dropping off me and Jai at the restaurant? I need some boxes moved around. Want to take advantage of muscles here," Sonny added.

"Oh, I can help," Reena said.

"No, Jai's fine," Sonny quickly answered. "I'm sure you have spreadsheets to look at. Or something."

"No problem," answered Akash. He caught Sonny's eyes in the rearview. His message was clear. *Don't mess this up!*

Her brothers got out at The Masala Hut to much thanks and promises to do it again. She started to get out. "I can walk from here."

"It's fine. I'm going past the hotel anyway."

"Okay." Reena sat back down. "I had a great time today," she told him.

The fact that she had enjoyed herself made him ridiculously happy. "Me, too. This is nice."

"What?"

"This. You and me. Friends," he said.

"It is," she answered, a huge smile on her lips. "Let's not forget your end of the deal."

"I won't. I did talk to my mom, though."

"See, you're learning." She grinned.

He drove her to the hotel and pulled up in the back lot. "I'm having dinner at Asha's. My mom and Kirti will be there. Official meeting of Nila's girlfriend. They may be ready to propose."

"OMG! That's so awesome!"

"It is. Priya is a sweetheart. Mom will be so happy."

"Nila has always seemed like a sweet person. Tell her I'm happy for her."

"Is that all?" he asked.

"Why? What else is there?"

"You don't want to offer Lulu's as a wedding venue?"

She looked almost hurt that he had asked. "First. Contrary to what recent events have portrayed, I am capable of being a human being, and of simply being happy for someone without searching out my angle. Second. I highly doubt Nila would be interested in doing anything with Lulu's after what happened with Asha."

Akash just looked at her. After a small silence, she started to get out of the car. "I'm sorry," he said.

"For what?"

"For assuming you had an angle in your happiness for Nila. For not hearing you out the night everything went down with Asha." He looked at her, making sure he caught her eye. This was for real. "I owed it to you to at least hear what you had to say about it." He shook his head. "It's no excuse, but the reality is that every relationship, except for Asha and Nila, that I have, usually ends in the person leaving me at some point." He paused. "I suppose there was a part of me just waiting for you to leave. So, I left you first."

Reena just stared at him. "What are you saying?"

He stared back at her. What was he saying? Was he saying that he still loved her? He had no right. But that didn't mean it wasn't true. "I'm saying…that I'm sorry.

I'm saying that for whatever it's worth, Reena, that …
I still love you. That I never stopped loving you."

She stared at him, blank faced for a whole minute
before she finally spoke. "No. No." She shook her head,
as her voice got angrier. "No. You do not get to say that
right now." She fumbled with the door handle before
getting out of the car. She stood in the doorway, bent
over to look at him. "You do not get to *say* you still
love me when you have *shown* that you have no faith
in me. That you do not believe in me." She raised her
voice. "That you never believed in me."

"What are you talking about?"

"I'm talking about secret dealings with my father
to 'save' Lulu's, when you knew—" Her voice broke
and her breath hitched, and her eyes filled with angry
tears. "You, more than anyone else, you knew that I
was doing everything in my power to save Lulu's myself." She slammed the door and stomped off.

"Reena!" He called after her.

She held up her hand to stop him, but didn't turn
back as she stormed off.

"I wasn't trying to save Lulu's," Akash said to her
back.

Chapter Thirty-Four

Honestly. She slammed his car door shut and rushed to the back door of the hotel. The absolute complete gall of that man! Just when she was getting comfortable with him. Enjoying this new type of connection. Just when she thought she might actually be able to work with him for a year.

He had to ruin it all by saying he loved her. And her stupid, misguided heart, melting like chocolate over a flame when he said it. No. She steeled herself against her own heart, because if he knew her at all, he never would have tried to save Lulu's *for her*.

She swiped herself in and headed to her room. Halfway there, she turned and went to the elevator. She couldn't go to her room right now. Not to where she and Akash had been together.

She pushed the button for the office floor. It might be Sunday, but she needed to get to the work schedule. Work would calm her, distract her from warm and fuzzy romantic things handsome men said when they really should not.

Reena grabbed her laptop and settled in on her sofa. She opened the dreaded work schedule. She stared at it a moment, then began typing in the search bar.

Requirements for teaching business.

Where can I teach business?

Who benefits from teaching business?

Maybe it was silly, but she had really enjoyed helping people get started in business. According to Google, her master's degree in business qualified her to teach.

"You know. The Women's Giving Circle is always looking for people to run workshops that educate underserved women." Kirti had come in and was peering over her shoulder.

"Damn, girl. I did not hear you come in," Reena said, her hand over her rapidly beating heart.

Kirti shrugged, still looking at her computer. "You were engrossed." She nodded at the screen. "Although, I'm not sure how much, if anything, they pay."

"I don't need to get paid," Reena said.

Kirti reached over and typed and clicked. "Apply here."

Reena grinned. "I will." She started the application and then halted a second. "Why are you here? Something up?"

"No. I was just working some numbers, to see how much more staff we could hire."

"And?" Reena raised an eyebrow.

"And," the young woman grinned with what could only be a sense of pride, "I think we can hire what we need, especially with the restaurant opening soon."

"That's what I thought." Reena squeezed her hand. "We could not have done it without you."

"Or my brother's money," Kirti added.

"True." Reena agreed slowly, her irritation ramping up at him again. "As much as I don't want it to be true, it is."

"What's the big deal? It's still your place. You know this hotel like no one else. You have a vision for its future. You care about this hotel because it's your family. Money cannot buy that." Kirti pressed her lips together in a small shrug.

"But I kind of want to be able to do it on my own. Without help."

"Sure there's something to be said about that. But haven't you heard the saying, it takes a village?"

"That's just for raising children." Reena waved a hand.

"It doesn't have to be." Kirti shrugged. "Who said it doesn't take a village to be successful?"

"My mom and dad did it alone," Reena said.

"No. They didn't." Kirti frowned. "I read about them. They had help from friends, investors, everyone."

"How did you get so wise at such a young age?" Reena marveled at her.

Kirti smiled, half bashful, half smug. "It's a talent. And I read—a lot."

"Well, it's a talent I would like to have beside me," Reena said. "If you were ever interested."

"What do you mean?" Kirti's eyes widened, and she seemed to freeze in her spot.

"When do you graduate?"

"December."

"Okay. When you graduate, if you want a real job here, getting paid and everything, come see me. We'll talk."

Kirti jumped away from the sofa. "Are you serious? You better not be kidding me? This is not because Akash is like my stepbrother?"

"This is in spite of the fact that he is your stepbrother." Reena chuckled.

"Oh my god!" Kirti bent over and hugged Reena's neck. "I am interested. It's all I ever wanted!"

Reena reached her arm over to hug Kirti's neck. "It's yours. But do have something else in your life. Trust me."

"Is that what this teaching thing is about?"

Reena looked at the young woman. "It is."

"I'll keep it in mind." Kirti sighed. "Okay, I'm headed out."

"Big dinner with the family tonight, huh?" Reena said.

"How did you know?"

"Akash mentioned it."

"Did he, now?" Kirti mused. "Huh. What is the deal with you two?"

"No deal." Reena feigned interest in her computer screen. "We work together."

"Uh-huh. I work with people, but I do not look at them the way you two look at each other."

"Bye, Kirti! Have fun!" Reena smiled at Kirti as she left.

She finished her application, then did more research before finally hitting the work schedule. She needn't have worried about it; Kirti had done an excellent job of it all and it was ready to go for tomorrow.

She stretched and headed down to her room. She was getting off the elevator in the lobby when she bumped into Nicole and another woman she didn't know.

"Ms. Pandya," Nicole said. "Have you seen Mr. Gupta?"

"I believe that he is with his family. Have you called?"

"It's Sunday night so I did not," Nicole explained.

"What's going on? I'll try to help." Reena went on high alert.

"It's about the mold," the other woman said.

Reena's eyes flew open. "Mold? Where?" Her heart thudded in her chest. What mold?

"In the ballroom," Nicole informed her, matter-of-factly.

"Mr. Gupta, he knew about this mold?" Reena could not believe her ears.

"He's the one who called in Lorraine." Nicole indicated the woman next to her.

"What do you do, Lorraine?"

"I'm the mold remediator."

"Is that so?" Reena said as she pulled out her phone and all-caps texted him.

Akash left Reena, deciding to forego his work. What had he been thinking, blurting out his feelings like that? And the look on her face. She had been appalled.

The elevator doors to Asha's loft opened, and Akash found himself in the company of his mother and her husband, as well as Asha, Nila, Priya and her parents, and of course his father. Seeing him reminded Akash that he still needed to tell his father that he was leaving Gupta Equity.

Akash greeted his mother with a hug. He had missed too many and wasn't going to miss any more. Nila was glowing as she chatted with Priya and her parents. Akash hugged his sister and met Priya's parents, who looked at Nila with as much love as they looked at Priya. It warmed Akash's heart to see his sister so loved.

Asha served a round of prosecco while they waited for Kirti to arrive. "I'll be happy when she finishes this internship with that hotel," Asha said. "That Reena works her too hard." Clearly Asha had yet to forgive Reena for trying to keep Rahul's infidelity from her.

"I think Kirti is enjoying her time," Akash observed. "She says she's making a difference."

"How do you know?" Asha asked.

"Uh, well." He hadn't told his sister that he was the one who had given money to Lulu's. And Kirti did not talk about her work at Lulu's because she didn't want ot upset Asha. "Kirti and I had lunch."

The elevator door dinged and the woman herself walked out. "I'm sorry. Did I miss anything?"

"No," Nila said smiling at her. "But now that everyone is here." She took Priya's hand and they beamed at each other. "Priya proposed last night, and I said yes!" Both women held out their left hands which were now adorned with gorgeous diamond rings.

The family cheered and clapped for them. Akash hugged them both tight, filled with happiness for his sister and her fiancée. "I'm super excited to get another sister." He said as he hugged her. "But I guess that means yet another Raksha Bandhan gift I need to get. That makes four." He glanced at Kirti.

Kirti grinned at him. "You'll have to make up for the years you missed."

Akash was laughing, enjoying himself in the moment. He had temporarily pushed aside the fact that he had blurted out his heart to Reena and she had gotten pissed. It was not like him to be so rash. Maybe that talk with his mom got to him. Maybe because Nila and Priya were getting engaged.

Maybe it was simply because he loved her. Everyone was chattering and calling restaurants. Within minutes, his father had a large enough reservation for them all to celebrate over a dinner.

"Thank you, Dad," Nila said, hugging him.

Their father hugged Priya then Nila. "It's the least I can do, huh?"

They all started piling into the elevator when

Akash's phone dinged. A text from Reena. MOLD?
WHY DIDN'T YOU TELL ME?

Oh, shit.

Chapter Thirty-Five

"Okay. Let's go see what's what." Reena nodded at Nicole and Lorraine, and they led the way as they spoke.

"I'm sorry I don't have better news for you," Lorraine started. "But the mold is in half the floor and most of the walls. Remediation is going to take time. I can do my part quickly, but everything has to dry. We're not in the humidity of summer, so that helps. But Maryland weather seems most unpredictable during the seasonal transitions, and that's where we are in late October."

"What time frame are we talking?" asked Reena as they reached the ballroom. She gasped at the sight. The carpet was ripped up, revealing black underneath. The walls had many holes in them. Even without mold remediation, these two rooms would need at least a month if not more to be presentable.

Tears burned at her backs of her eyes, as she realized that not only would she not be able to host the Shah wedding ceremony, the guests would have to be diverted to another location to stay as well.

Lorraine was still explaining what needed to be done. Reena forced herself to focus on her voice. She nodded. "Okay. Yes, let's do it. We have no choice."

Reena stood there, numb, trying to do the math in her head. The loss of the wedding and the guests. The few guests they had currently coming in the upcoming week would be informed and offered rooms on higher floors. But they would likely opt to cancel and book elsewhere.

She picked up her phone to text Kirti. But it was late and Kirti was celebrating her sister. This could wait until morning.

"The remediation will be done fairly quickly—you'll only be down about a week—it's the drying and the fixing up that will take time," Lorraine continued. "It's the next few days or so, you want to be careful down here," she said softly.

Reena nodded her head as if all of that was fine with her. But it wasn't. None of it was. She cleared her throat. "When can you start?"

Lorraine grinned at her. "For Mr. Gupta, we start tomorrow morning."

"What do you mean?"

"Mr. Gupta is the reason I have my business." She

said it as if Reena should know what she was talking about.

Reena shook her head to indicate that she had no idea what she was talking about. This was the second company that credited Akash with helping them.

"Mr. Gupta is part of the group Angel Investors. They pool some money together, to help businesses with potential. I got my start from the money from the Angel Investors." She nodded at the other woman. "So did Nicole. And Elijah as well."

"So, he gives you money and you're at his beck and call?"

"Oh no, Hon. It's not like that. We help him out because that is how we show our gratitude. To be honest, Mr. Gupta has never called us before. This is the first time," Nicole explained.

"He's a good man." Lorraine looked around the ballroom. "I'll bring out a crew first thing tomorrow morning. We'll get this sealed off and get started." She looked at Reena. "If you're okay with that."

"I am," Reena managed. She looked around the ballroom and walked out.

She was going to have to call Mrs. Shah in the morning. She had colleagues in town who would honor the rate the guests had paid to Lulu's in a situation like this. Reena had done it for them in the past. What she needed was a venue for the wedding. She glanced at her phone. Nine at night. Too late to really be calling anyone just now. She texted Sangeeta that she needed to talk to her ASAP, but not to say anything to Mrs Shah.

Reena woke tired and frustrated. Mrs. Shah was

going to have to be dealt with, but first, she needed a venue. Sangeeta had not texted back. Reena got up and went for her run, stopping of course at The Masala Hut.

"Where's Sangeeta?" Reena asked over her piping-hot chai.

Sonny was doing five things at once as per usual in his kitchen. "Uh… I don't know. I don't even know what time it is. Just text her." Sonny barked an order at a new face in the kitchen, so Reena quietly slipped out and finished her run, ending up back at Lulu's.

She texted Sangeeta, asking her to call ASAP. Next she called the owner/manager of The Posh. She and Tressa were frenemies, working in the same business, but direct competitors. Reena had more or less stolen Asha Gupta's wedding from The Posh. Tressa would likely still be upset. But then, seeing how all that worked out—or didn't—Tressa might be happy to gloat. And maybe help Reena.

After a draining fifteen-minute conversation with Tressa, who spent eleven of those minutes gloating, Reena was no closer to a new wedding venue than she had been before. She showered and headed up to her office. Any number of things awaited her. She made a detour to the ballrooms.

Sure enough, Lorraine and a large crew of men and women were sealing off the ballroom as they prepped for remediation.

It was here that she found Akash. He was wearing the dark jeans again with a crewneck shirt and blazer. He was deep in conversation with Lorraine, who was gesturing around as if explaining to Akash.

As if he sensed her presence, Akash lifted his face to her just as she approached. She honestly hated how handsome he was. And that look on his face, like he was ready to get on his knees and beg her forgiveness. Well, maybe she liked that.

Lorraine turned and saw her, and then nodded to Akash as he stepped away from her and Reena made her way to him.

"Reena. I was going to tell you. I was just—"

"Just what? Going to take care of it?" she snapped.

"Well." He furrowed his brow. "Yes. I was."

Reena opened her mouth, a protest at the ready. But what was she protesting? That Akash was going to use his ample resources to get Lulu's fixed as efficiently as possible? He couldn't exactly keep that a secret from her, so he wasn't hiding anything.

Huh.

"I was just waiting for Lorraine's assessment of the time, because I knew you would want to know that because—"

"The Shah wedding," she said quietly.

He nodded. "Yes."

Silence floated between them during which Reena was quite irritated with Akash, but she wasn't quite sure why. Not true. Her irritation was due to the fact that she was not in control of the situation. That Lulu's had been taken care of without her. Someone else in the "village" had fixed things.

Oh, and he'd said he loved her.

"So…we're good?" he asked.

"Looks that way." But damn, she wanted to be mad

at him. Thankfully, her phone buzzed. Sangeeta. "I need to take this." She tapped and put her phone to her ear, as Akash nodded. She stepped away.

"Sangeeta. I need another venue for the Shah wedding. And don't ask me why, because I don't want to tell you."

"What? Why?" Came the puzzled reply.

"Because of your loyalty to your clients. Just treat me like the crazy sister of your boyfriend," Reena said.

"Ugh. Reena…"

"Do you know of any venues?" Reena asked again.

"Well, there's always that new boutique hotel, The Epic. They just opened, so they may have some openings," Sangeeta offered.

"Thanks." The name sounded familiar. "You are the best, Sangeeta."

"Wait—what's going—"

"Oops—can't hear you. Bye." She tapped off the phone and turned to Akash. "Sangeeta suggested The Epic. Why is that name so familiar?"

Akash grinned at her. "Because you're going to a wedding there this Saturday as my date."

"I am?" She racked her brain and pulled up her calendar on her phone, and sure enough there it was. "I am." She stared at him a minute. "Oh, the scary aunties. I remember." She rolled her eyes and chuckled. "No worries." She paused and looked at him. "It's not a real date, right?"

He nodded at her. "Of course not. Fake as they come. I just don't like dealing—"

"With the aunties." She nodded. "Okay. Fine."

"Reena, listen. About what I said last night—" He stepped closer.

She put her hand up. "You know what? I can't right now. Maybe I'm a workaholic, but there's too much to do with Mrs. Shah and the restaurant..."

"Of course." He smiled, but she knew it was forced. It seemed he had many different smiles as well.

"It's probably best we stay business colleagues, anyway. Every time I let my guard down, my business suffers. And we both know I can't have that."

"No. Certainly not," Akash replied.

"I mean, we tried it as a couple, and that fell apart—even as friends, it's too hard. We are forced to be business partners, so we'll finish out the year, and with hard work, I'll be able to buy you out next year. And then we can go our separate ways."

Akash nodded in agreement. "We're just not relationship people, right?" Sadness oozed from him.

She nodded. "So it seems."

On their second incredible night in Vegas, they had ordered room service and a bottle of champagne in the middle of the night. To "fuel up" as Akash had said.

"You ever been in a long-term relationship?" Reena had asked as she popped a fry in her mouth. "I'm just curious. Because it occurs to me that I am twenty-six and I never have been, but more importantly, I do not care."

"Define long-term." He took a fry as well. She had donned his dress shirt and all he had on were his boxers as they sat at the edge of the bed in front of the room service table.

She got off the bed and rummaged through her bag. "Uh. I don't know. Like longer than six months and you weren't bored." She came back and sat down on the bed and opened the small packet she had pulled from her bag.

"What's that?"

"Hot sauce. For the fries."

He had smiled and nodded his head. "Good call. By that definition, no. I'm usually really busy with work—"

"And they get upset you won't hang out every night."

"Yes." He agreed. "And to be honest, I don't really know if forever is a real thing."

She had shrugged. "It's a thing—my parents have been together forever—and they still like each other. I just don't know if it's my thing."

They dipped their fries into the hot sauce and finished them off.

"I don't think it's my thing," he had said. "What's in that bowl?"

She had lifted the wrapping off the bowl and let the shirt fall open as she raised herself to kneeling on the bed. "Whipped cream."

"Of course," he murmured as he knelt in front of her and scooped some whipped cream into his hand. "I've never known a woman who had hot sauce in her bag, and then ordered whipped cream for fun."

"I need you to do something," Reena said to him, shaking the memory from her head. "As a business partner."

"What's that?" His mouth was pressed shut and he

looked at her, sadness in his normally amused dark eyes. Maybe he recalled the same memory.

"Call Mrs. Shah. Proactively. Turn on the charm or FaceTime her so she can see your handsome face. Whatever it takes for her not to call me until Sunday. After we go to that wedding."

"You think I'm charming?" He tried to be light and flirty, but he fell short, and his disappointment shone through.

She ignored it. "What matters is that Mrs. Shah finds you charming."

Chapter Thirty-Six

Saturday seemed to drag in its arrival. Between celebrating Nila and Priya and his mom planning an impromptu and quick engagement party to take place on the *Asha-Nila*, the mold in the ballrooms, the new chef setting up the kitchen and Reena's stress level, he thought Saturday would never arrive.

His original reason for asking Reena still stood. This was a family friend of his mother, and all of the aunties were going to be in matchmaking mode. Asha would be given a pass, since she just suffered all that Rahul drama. Nila was newly engaged, so that left him. Hopefully, with Reena at his side, he would be able to neatly sidestep all the questions, and just enjoy the evening. The bonus reason had been that he would get to spend some non-office time with Reena. But Reena had been clear about her intentions, and this week there had been no evidence of her changing her mind.

He had begged off of going to the mehndi and the grah shanti, but they were invited to the ceremony and the reception. Reena was thrilled because that meant she could scope out more of the place. She had been expertly avoiding Mrs. Shah's calls, by having him return them.

He had spent the better part of the past couple days keeping Mrs. Shah from coming to Lulu's.

Asha had brought him clothes, though she had been less than impressed with his new apartment.

"It's functional, Asha. The water works, the oven and stove work, lights stay on and there's AC," he explained to her. "I don't really need all the fancy stuff."

"But the fancy stuff is nice. This is like a quarter of the size of your condo and the carpet is ugly." Asha looked around, her distaste clear on her face. "The view was awesome there."

That was true. "It's fine. I'm fine."

"Why did you even move? Why sell the condo?" she asked as she had hung up his sherwani in his closet (it was not a walk-in). She had chosen a sage-green color, with no beading, simple cream pants and a scarf.

"I needed a change."

She had rolled her eyes at him as she left. "Wear the scarf," she had commanded as she walked out.

Fortunately, they were blessed with a pleasant fall day in October, otherwise, Akash would have roasted in the outfit. He dressed and threw the scarf around his neck, before calling an Uber to Lulu's, so he and Reena could Uber over together.

Akash texted her when he got close. He got out of the car and went to wait for her in the lobby of Lulu's. He didn't have to wait long. She came bustling toward him from the elevator bays. She was resplendent.

Her usual ponytail gave way for her long tresses to be free with a slight wave to them. She was wearing a cream choli with minimal beading and a sheer sage-green-colored dupatta which she had draped over her like a sari. Her midriff was half bare, and the choli and chaniya hugged her curves like skin. His heart raced just seeing her. He inhaled and exhaled slowly to calm the traitorous organ.

Maybe seeing her every day would numb his reaction to her.

Maybe…not.

She approached him with a crooked smile on her face. "We match. What are the odds?"

He shrugged. "Asha says that sage green is *the* color right now."

"Does she?" Reena asked, her brow furrowed. Then she shrugged it off. "Well Asha always knows the trends." She stood looking at him.

He could not take his eyes off her.

"Stop looking at me like that," Reena said softly.

"Like what?"

"You know. Like you…" She glanced around the lobby.

"Like I love you?"

"Yes." She looked up at him. "We can't have that," she said, her voice low but firm.

"But it's true."

"I told you, we're not—you know what? Never mind. Not discussing this. I need to focus on the venue. Call the Uber and let's just get this over with."

"Fine," he said.

"Fine."

He checked his phone. "Uber's here."

She led the way to the car, he opened the door for her and she got in. Akash slid in next to her. The ride was relatively short, but they used the time to get caught up on all the hotel stuff while they rode over.

"Ishani and Sonny have started working together. Just to give Ishani a sense of how a professional kitchen is run," Reena told him.

He stared at her a beat. They were really going to do this. They were going to be business partners. Nothing else. Fine. "Kirti mentioned that she has two people to work in the kitchen," Akash reported as if he were reporting to his father, clinically. No emotion.

She flicked her gaze to him at his change in tone, but she hardly skipped a beat. "Perfect. That'll get us started. Then we can add as we go along."

"My thoughts exactly."

The Uber pulled up to the hotel and Akash got out and extended his hand to Reena to help her out. She looked up at him, her lips pressed together, and he was sure she was going to eschew his offer and get out on her own. To his surprise, she took his hand and allowed him to help her out of the car. They started for the door, and she entwined her fingers with his. He stopped and looked at her.

"You want it to look real, don't you?" she said, her tone businesslike.

"Of course." He answered as he squeezed her hand in his.

Chapter Thirty-Seven

Reena could not help it. Reena was enjoying being Akash Gupta's fake girlfriend. There were probably a hundred reasons for her not to enjoy being any kind of his girlfriend, the primary one being that she had meant what she had said earlier in the week. They were only good together as business partners. Neither of them seemed cut out for that long-term relationship business.

She had to remind herself of their *partnership* as she noted how he filled out that sherwani. Honestly, Reena felt sorry for the groom; she was sure even he would pale in comparison to Akash. "Let's find seats—the ceremony's starting soon." They walked into the ceremony hall together.

She leaned toward him. "Good size. The vendor has

provided a beautiful mandap." She glanced around. "Chairs are comfy and the staff is attentive." She grinned up at him. "You think Mrs. Shah would approve?"

"Possibly."

"As long as you present it well, it'll be fine," she teased him. "My concern is really the JFL retreat. I'd rather not have them dodging mold."

"Agreed," he said. "Maybe I can convince my father to lend us the boat?"

Her eyes lit up. "That would be perfect."

"I'll see what I can do."

The ceremony was lovely; the young couple were clearly in love. They threw flower petals as the couple walked back down the aisle to cheering and laughter. They cleared the hall and went outside to the garden for cocktail hour.

Reena was chatting with a young woman who attended college with Kirti, when Akash approached her and handed her a drink. An extra dirty vodka martini. Her drink of choice.

"Hi." He extended his hand to the young woman. "I'm Akash, Kirti's brother."

Melissa looked confused but shook his hand all the same. "Melissa. Nice to meet you. Kirti never mentioned—"

"It's a long story." Akash shrugged. "But I finally came to my senses."

Kirti popped by just then. "Hey, Melissa. You'll never guess who Rani brought with her?"

Melissa's eyes widened. "Not Param?"

The name rang a bell for Reena, but she couldn't place it. Kirti nodded conspiratorially. Melissa turned to Akash and Reena. "Excuse me."

"Of course," they said in unison and the two young women took off.

"Thanks." She raised her glass to him. "How did you know?"

"How did I know what your drink was?" He raised an eyebrow at her and blew air from his mouth. "Please."

"You were paying attention." She could not help the small smirk that came over her face. "Well, that was very *kind* of you." Warm and fuzzy feelings spread throughout her body at the thought.

The first time Akash had opened a door for her, she had turned on him.

"I am perfectly capable of opening my own door," she had snapped.

"Of course, you are. But it's kind. I would open the door for a man, a woman, a child regardless of whether I perceived them able to do so or not."

She had been taken aback. "So, you're just being nice?"

"Yes."

"Who does that?"

"I do."

He laughed softly at her use of the word *kind*, and then raked his gaze over yet again.

"Are you okay? You're acting like you never saw

a woman in a chaniya-choli before," she said as she sipped her drink.

"I haven't." His eyes never left her. "Not until just this moment."

She felt herself heating and melting, but remembered that they were role-playing right now. "Pretty smooth. Though no one's here to hear you say it."

"You're here. You heard me." His gaze was devastatingly intense. Had he forgotten they were just business partners?

She gulped at her drink. "It's a great line. You'll have to use it on the next woman."

"There won't be a next woman."

She snapped her gaze to him.

"Don't look at me like that. Neither one of us had interest in being in any kind of long-term relationship before we…met. That hasn't changed for me. Six months. You were the longest relationship I ever had. It's you or no one."

He wasn't wrong. Those nights in Vegas, Reena had experienced a connection with Akash that she had not had before. She had looked at couples in awe, wondering how it was possible to maintain a relationship. Not that she hadn't seen her parents be business partners as well as husband and wife all these years. But in her opinion, they were the exception, not the rule.

She stared at him a moment, speechless. Her shock passed, and a small smile took its place. "You look pretty amazing yourself tonight." She opened her mouth like she had more to say, but then snapped it shut.

"Akash." A couple aunties approached, curiosity

oozing from them. Both women eyed Reena, and one addressed Akash. "Who have we here?"

Akash cleared his throat. "Malti Auntie, this is Reena Pandya."

"Reena. How nice to meet you," Malti Auntie simpered before turning to Akash. "Well, it seems I'll have to find a different match for my Lena."

Akash flushed in that moment, and Reena had never seen anything so completely amusing. Not to mention the urge she suddenly had to find out who the hell this Lena was to him.

"It was nice seeing you, Auntie." To steer her away from Malti Auntie, Akash placed his hand on her lower back. Reena could not remember ever feeling safer or more secure than in that moment. She stiffened her back so as to push the feeling away.

"Who's Lena?" she asked. Clearly, she couldn't even wait until they had privacy.

"She's the woman I dated for three months. Before you," Akash offered without hesitation.

"What happened?"

"We just both lost interest. She's intelligent, beautiful, super fun." He chuckled. "She was *a lot* of fun."

Reena hated her instantly.

He shrugged. "But we got to the three-month point, and there just wasn't any connection left there. It was a mutual parting." He looked at her. "Jealous?"

"Of course not." She retorted back quickly. "Don't you remember me saying we were better as business partners? We're friends. Friends can talk about exes and things, and it's fine." She was rambling; she bit the inside of her cheek to shut herself up.

Chapter Thirty-Eight

"Oh," Reena gasped beside him. "It's Conner Smith, the owner of The Epic. I'm going to meet him." She took a couple steps and turned back to him. "Did you want to come?"

"No. I'm sure you'll handle it better than me."

"You are the primary owner," she said.

"It's your hotel, Reena. Only you can have this conversation." Akash had raised his glass to her and she held up crossed fingers and went on her way.

Akash busied himself catching up with old friends, periodically glancing over to where Reena and Conner were chatting. After about fifteen minutes, he saw them shake hands and Reena turned and scanned the room. She was looking for him. It should not have sent a thrill through his body, but it did.

He watched and waited for her to find him. When she caught his eye, she broke out into a huge smile and walked toward him. As she got closer, he saw the excitement on her face. It was contagious.

He handed her drink back to her. She was giddy. "He said yes. Plus we're going to set up a cooperative agreement in which our hotels would be able to act like sister hotels, as opposed to competitors."

"That's awesome!" he said.

Reena was going over the details of what she and Conner had discussed when a woman came to them.

"Excuse me—I was told that you are Reena Pandya?"

"I am." Reena shot a questioning glance at him. He shrugged. He had no idea who this woman was.

The woman extended her hand to Reena. "I wanted to introduce myself. I'm Monica Lopez." Reena's eyes widened at the name. "I am in charge of setting up speakers and workshops for the Women's Giving Circle in this area."

Reena shook the offered hand. "I'm so happy to meet you. Kirti Doshi must have sent you."

"That she did." Monica smiled. "I saw your application and I would love to have you teach a workshop. I have already sent you an email, but I wanted to say hello in person. Such a small world—I had no idea you were part of the Gupta family."

Reena flushed. "Oh. No. I'm not a part of the family."

"Oh, but you certainly will be—isn't that right,

Reena?" Malti Auntie had sauntered past at just that moment.

Reena rallied seamlessly. "Of course." She giggled and laid a hand on Akash's forearm. "Nothing official, however."

Monica stepped back. "In any case, it was wonderful meeting you. And I hope to hear from you soon."

"Absolutely." Reena nearly glowed with excitement.

Once Monica Lopez was out of earshot, she turned to him and actually squealed with delight. "Did you hear that? She wants me to teach a workshop. I mean, I applied on a whim. I thought maybe I could teach, you know? That it might be fun to have something outside of the hotel, like you have sailing. But I didn't think they'd actually want me. Or that I would meet Monica Lopez in person."

She had said all of that without taking a breath. There was a glow on her cheeks and a glaze in her eye that he hadn't seen before. She had been squeezing his arm this whole time, and her excitement was contagious.

Akash found himself grinning and nodding his head along with her, though he had no idea what she was talking about. "You applied to teach?" He asked when she stopped to breathe.

"Well, I forgot to tell you with all the hotel drama. But yes—and she just said she wants me." Reena was like teenager at prom.

"I was here. I saw." He nodded. "So very proud of you." And without thinking, he leaned in and kissed her temple. She must not have been thinking either, because she leaned in to him for just a moment, then she seemed to remember herself, and pulled back.

How was he supposed to get through the next year working with her? More to the point, how was he going to get through this wedding? It was a testament to his level of discomfort that he was relieved when his father approached, another couple accompanying him.

"Ah. Here he is." His father beamed. "Eric and Sejal Pierson, meet my son, Akash Gupta."

Akash shook the extended hands. "So nice to meet you, Uncle, Auntie. This is Reena Pandya."

"His girlfriend." Reena shook their hands.

His father did a double take at Reena, but then turned back to him. "Akash, Eric and Sejal are going to be partnering with Gupta Equity, right around the time you become a partner."

"I'm not going to become a partner." The words just fell from his mouth as if he'd been dying to say them. Which, he realized, he was.

His father's grin faltered as he turned to look at him. Then he laughed. "He jokes. My son."

"No. Dad. I'm not joking. I'm not becoming a partner."

"What?"

"I'm saying that I sold my shares in Gupta when I sold the condo and my car." Akash found himself to be surprisingly calm as he broke this news to his father. Meanwhile, Reena had taken his hand again, her small strong fingers entwined with his, supporting him.

The Piersons, sensing drama, quietly excused themselves. His father stared at him, disbelieving. Akash could see his father's brain trying to make sense of it all. When it clicked into place, Pradeep Gupta's face darkened.

"That's where you got all that money to buy that hotel." He flicked his gaze to Reena. "Pandya Hotels is Lulu's Boutique Hotel."

Reena's fingers stiffened in his hand and he heard her gasp.

"I'd heard rumors that there was a group of investors, calling themselves the Angel Investors—you neglected to mention that you're part of that group." His father was angry. "What will you do now? Run that hotel?"

"Why don't I come to the office tomorrow, and we can discuss this then." Akash spoke softly.

"You brought it up," his father barked. "This happened over three months ago and you decide that this wedding is the place to bring it up. So let's discuss this now. Let's discuss your betrayal, your abandonment of your father. Everything I did was for you and your sisters."

"That's not true and you know it." Akash fired up instantly. "Whatever you did, you did for you. I did this for me. So I could be my own person."

"You should have been upfront with me. Why wait three months?"

Why had he waited so long? What held him back? He knew now. "I didn't want to hurt you. I didn't want you to feel abandoned. If you don't have me, you're alone," Akash said.

"I'm fine. And I'm not alone," his father spat at him.

But he was; Akash knew it, and on some level, his father knew it, too.

"What is all the commotion going on here?" Asha came over, her voice even but with a hint of warning, a smile plastered onto her face. "You're making a scene, Dad."

"Did you know that your brother sold all his shares at Gupta, his million-dollar condo and his car, so he could put that money into Lulu's Boutique Hotel?" He shook his head as if running a hotel was beneath him and Akash.

"That's ridiculous," Asha said. "Bhaiya would never put money into that woman's—" Asha stopped as she seemed to just now notice Reena standing next to him. She snapped her head to him. "What the—"

"I can explain, Asha," Akash started. No sooner were the words out of his mouth than he felt Reena's fingers loosen their grip. He squeezed her fingers, hoping she wouldn't let go.

His sister stared at him, her voice ramping up, no longer cool or calm. "She was going to let me marry a cheater. No, she was just going to let me go through the whole prewedding fiasco so she could save her hotel. That was the hotel that you gave money to?"

"I invested in it, Asha," he began to explain.

"Why? Why would you do that?"

He stared at his sister. "Because, Asha, I'm in love with her."

Asha's jaw dropped for an instant. "It's her, isn't it? Reena Pandya. She's the secret girlfriend you had all along." Asha was close to hysterical. If their father had caused a scene, this was beyond that. Everyone nearby was watching Asha. "She was dating you and she still threw me under the bus. And then you helped her by throwing money at her hotel?" Asha shook her head. "Bhaiya. You have got to be kidding me. I'm your sister. How could you?"

"Hey, Asha Ben." Nila came up. "Take it down a notch, huh?"

"He broke up with me," Reena blurted out and she freed her hand from his. She was focused straight ahead at Asha and Nila. "You're right. We were secretly together. But that night, after I confessed to erasing that video, I went to his place." Her breath was choppy; she was close to falling apart. "And he broke up with me. Because I hurt you. So don't be mad at him. He's a great brother, and I was a lousy friend to you."

"Reena—" he started.

Her eyes were filled with tears. "It's okay. They're your family. I get that. I would protect my family, too." She leaned toward him and whispered. "You should have told me what you did. That you sold—" She swallowed hard and offered him a watery smile. "It doesn't matter." She turned and left.

Chapter Thirty-Nine

Reena walked as fast as her pointy heels would allow her, hoping to not cause a further scene as she walked out. She pulled out her phone and called the first person she thought of. Sangeeta.

"Hey, I'm at The Epic. Can you come get me?"

"Sure. You okay?"

"Not really." How could she be; she'd just realized that she was desperately in love with Akash Gupta, that he'd sold everything to invest in her because he had faith in her, not because he was saving her. Not that it mattered. She'd never have him, because his family would never have her.

"I'll be there in fifteen minutes."

Reena tapped her phone off and walked to the corner to wait for Sangeeta.

"Reena!" Akash reached her, out of breath. "Where are you going?"

"Home." She didn't even bother to wipe away her tears.

"Come with me. We'll go somewhere and talk—"

"I love you," she blurted out, the tears still coming. "I *really* hate that I love you, because it'll never work. But I do."

"Reena. Let's talk about this."

"What's there to talk about? I never expected to feel this way, ever. This feeling that I have—this longing to be with you all the time, whether we're working or playing or arguing." She gave a sardonic, teary laugh. "I really love arguing with you." She shook her head; she was ridiculous. Her parents hated arguing with each other. "This feeling that I belong to you… that somehow, I'm yours… I didn't think I was capable of feeling like that…of being so vulnerable. But then when I'm with you, I do a lot of things I never thought I'd be capable of—like sailing or teaching…or apologizing when I'm wrong. Love was never a priority. Not until I met you. Then I wanted it all, the wedding, marriage, a family. And I hate that because I only want those things with you. And I'll never have that because I'll never ask you to choose between me and your family." She paused for breath. "And then there's the money."

"Reena. It was supposed to be a surprise." Akash sighed. "For your big-getting-Lulu's-birthday. I knew you would be struggling with Lulu's even if Asha's wedding had brought in clients and guests…and I wanted to be a part of…the solution, of helping you get your dream. You had always talked about how your parents enjoyed working together. I knew you would never give up Lulu's, so I thought about how wonderful it would be if we—you and I—took over and ran Lulu's together. What would be better than working with the one you loved?" He was pleading with her with every part of his body. Begging her to believe him.

She did.

But it changed nothing.

Emotions and thoughts swirled through her; it was so heady to think that Akash wanted to follow her dream with her.

"Say something." Akash was nearly begging.

"I… I was so sure I knew you. I was so sure six months was enough to gauge who you really were. But you turned out to be someone I couldn't have even imagined. I could know you for six months or six lifetimes and continue to discover new and amazing parts of you." She paused as a new wave of tears burned behind her eyes. She didn't even try to stop them. "Who sells their home, and their birthright, to help someone else? Who does that? Certainly not me. No, *I* throw friends and loved ones under buses to save what I love. You were right to leave me that night. You and I are too different, too chaotic. All. The. Time. We were never going to last."

"Reena—" he started, his voice cracking.

Sangeeta, thank her perfect timing, pulled up just

then. "This is my ride." She opened the door and got in. Reena didn't bother with goodbye; she wouldn't have been able to say it.

Chapter Forty

"You should've stayed for the rest of the reception, Bhaiya." Kirti plopped herself onto his sofa next to Nila. He was cooking them dinner in his apartment.

"Your little scene was nothing compared to the drama between the bride's sister and the groom's brother," Nila started. "One of the aunties caught them doing it in a closet!"

"Honestly, they all had rooms in the hotel. Why didn't they just go to one of their rooms?" Kirti mused.

"Because, dear sister, sometimes, you just have to do it. Right there. Right then." Nila smirked.

Kirti sat straight up and faced Nila. "Do tell."

Nila smiled. "Well, this one time—"

"No." Akash had to intervene. He did not need to hear about his sister's sex life. "No. I draw the line."

The girls laughed. "You're so easy, Bhaiya," Nila said. "Mmm. What smells so good?"

"I'm trying to make Mom's pakora," he said. "So, the bride's sister and the groom's brother did not get caught having sex in a closet?"

"Oh. They did. Malti Auntie caught them. It was a whole thing. But the point is, no one cared about your little shouting match with Dad and Asha," Kirti explained.

"But Asha didn't come here, did she?" He mixed the chickpea flour with spices and water to make the batter.

His sisters exchanged a look. "Give her time—she'll come around," Nila said. "It's only been like three days."

"But even if she doesn't come around, Bhaiya. You have to live your life. People make mistakes. No one is perfect. Are you seriously going to let Ms. Pandya go because Asha is pissed?" Kirti said. "You haven't even come to work." She peeked at his batter. "Mom adds Cream of Wheat to make it more crispy."

"I can work from here. I spoke with Mrs. Shah. Explained about the mold. She's very happy to use The Epic. I believe Sangeeta is taking her for a tour," Akash said. He started slicing potatoes, onions and other vegetables.

Kirti looked at Nila. Nila nodded at her. "Bhaiya. Do you want to know?"

"Know what?"

"How Ms. Pandya is doing?" Kirti asked.

"We email." He made a pile of ring-cut onions.

Kirti shook her head. "That's work."

Akash stared at her. Of course he wanted to know how she was.

"I'll take that sad puppy dog look as a yes. She looks as bad as you. Well, maybe not as bad, since she's good with makeup. But she never smiles. She walks around in her power suits barking orders," Kirti reported. "The thing she's trying to fix right now is where to hold the JFL retreat."

"Bhaiya." Nila looked at him. "Family is tough. Everyone has difficult family members. But in the end, we all always love each other." She looked at his batter again. "But real love–that doesn't always come around. Think about it."

Chapter Forty-One

Thankfully the mold remediation was going as planned. The ballrooms would not be ready for renovation for at least a couple weeks. Her new agreement with The Epic was working beautifully. The Epic was willing to honor Lulu's rates for the rooms as well as the venues, so Mrs. Shah was getting the wedding she wanted for her daughter. She was so thrilled, she had sent her nieces to Reena.

Ishani had started to cook in Joy, lunch only for now, as the capacity of Lulu's was limited due to the remediation, but it was the perfect way for her to ease into the volume she would be cooking. She had already requested one more person to help cook. Kirti had searched her increasing database, and found a young single mother who could nicely fill that void.

Between all that and starting to choose carpet and such for the new ballrooms, Reena was busier than ever. She really shouldn't have time to think about Akash. Or miss him. Or notice that her heart ached for him.

But the cruel reality of a broken heart was that she could.

She was trying to lose herself in spreadsheets once again, when there was a knock at her door.

"Mom." She looked up and closed her laptop. Her mother hadn't come to the office in quite some time. "When did you and Dad get back?"

"Last night. We leave again in a couple days, but I heard you were moping around. So, I came to see you."

"James," Reena called out.

"Hmm?"

"Did you call my mother?"

"No." Pause. "Yes."

"I'm fine, Mom," Reena said.

"Of course you are." She smiled and came over to her desk. "You're not really the type to pine over a man, are you?"

"You know about Akash?"

She waved a hand. "I pieced it together. In any case, I just came here to tell you how proud of you I am for standing your ground."

"What?"

"Well, yes. I mean any man who undermines you and your abilities in a such a way—in any case, you have your focus back. No distractions in the shape of handsome, yet ultimately, useless men."

"He's not useless, and he didn't undermine me—he was acting out of..." Love. Sure, he could have discussed it with her. But people make mistakes, right? She certainly had made her share. She straightened and focused on what her mother was saying.

"...it's just better to be alone than to lose yourself to someone who doesn't understand you, and potentially lose your business. Okay, Beta?"

Movement behind her mother made her get up and her heart thudded in her chest at the sight of Akash standing in her doorway. Faded jeans, fitted navy T-shirt, she'd never seen him so casual at the office.

Her mother turned to see what had caught her attention and frowned upon seeing Akash enter the office.

"Auntie." He nodded at her mother as he walked in.

"Mr. Gupta," her mother answered. "I was just leaving." She leaned over and kissed Reena's cheek. "Remember what I said about focus." She nodded at Akash as she left.

"Hey." Reena somehow managed to make her voice work. She hadn't seen him for days and it simultaneously felt like forever and five minutes ago.

"Hey." He smiled and tilted his head toward the door where her mother had just left. "Not a fan of mine."

"She's not a fan of anything that she perceives takes my focus away from Lulu's." Reena breathed out.

Silence passed between them, during which Reena fought the urge to simply throw herself into his arms. "Uh. Mrs. Shah called. She's very happy—"

"I did not come here to talk about Mrs. Shah," Akash said, his eyes never leaving her face.

"Oh. Okay. What—"

He fixed his dark eyes on her, a small smile at those perfect lips. "I love you." His low rumble vibrated in her core.

Reena shook her head. "We've been through this. Asha—"

"No. You've been through this. Not me." He paused. "Forget Asha." He paused again. "I love you. I want to be with you. I want us to be together." He walked closer to her. "You and I are trying to figure who we are. But I already know. The person I want to be is the person I am when I'm with you. We do not have easy love, but you and I," he flicked a finger between them. "We wouldn't even know what to do with easy love. I heard what your mother said. I heard what Asha said." He stepped yet closer to her. "But weren't you the one who said that that was how family worked? People get upset, they get angry, but in the end, they love each other. That's family, you said."

"No one likes it when you use their own words against them." She half smiled at him, and he stepped close enough that she would hardly have to move to touch him.

"Amidst all that chaos, *we* work, because like it or not, we have become each other's family. Your mother, my sister—it's not perfect, but *we* love each other, *we* work. That night, I should have listened to you. There was a part of me that was so sure that you and I would end at some point, and I thought that was the moment. Forgive me and I will spend the rest of my life standing by your side, being there for you, loving you. Because we should not be apart. We're better together."

He'd done it. Been more vulnerable with Reena than he had ever been before. Laid his heart out for her. The past few days had been nothing but misery. The idea that they both loved each other, but were choosing to be apart because of outside circumstances. Yes, he loved Asha, but he wasn't going to sacrifice his happiness for her.

Reena was a good person. She was his person, and he wanted to be with her in whatever capacity she would allow.

At the moment, she was looking at him with confusion on her face. She was wearing the lavender suit today.

"You really love me. All parts of me. Even the complicated parts," she said.

"I love those parts the best." They were close enough that he could feel the heat from her body, smell the remnants of her perfume.

"I'll still argue with you," she whispered.

"Of course." He couldn't take his eyes off her.

"I'm bossy."

"That you are."

"I may not get it right every time."

"Me, either."

"I may stomp out and say I never want to see you again."

"I will chase you."

"I—"

He took her hands in his and lowered his face to hers, looking into her eyes. "Reena. I love you. And I want to be with you, come what may. The only question here is do you want to be with me?"

She pressed against him and brought her lips close to his. "I do."

His heart lifted and he closed the space between their lips to kiss the woman he loved.

A sharp knock at the door froze them.

"Well. Hello," Asha said from the doorway.

Reena froze midway to kissing Akash at the sound of his sister's voice. She glanced at him; he shrugged and moved to stand behind her.

"Asha," Reena said. "What a surprise."

Asha flicked her gaze to Akash, and then back to her. She looked sad. "I just came to...well. I have a boat," she said as if that explained everything.

Reena furrowed her brow. "Con-grat-u-lations?"

"The *Asha-Nila*? It's my boat. Technically, it's my dad's but my name is on the papers, so if I want, I can override him. And I heard you might need something for a retreat..." She tried to be casual about it. Apologies were clearly not her strong suit.

Something she had in common with Reena.

"Are you offering Lulu's the use of your boat?" Reena asked.

"It holds fifty people. If that helps, it's yours to borrow," she said.

"That would be great." Reena turned her head to Akash.

"Seriously, Asha?" He'd had no idea.

"It's perfect for the JFL retreat." Reena said before turning back to Asha. "I mean, just let me know the costs of fuel and manpower and whatever else. We can handle the rest. Thank you so much, Asha."

"Well." She bobbed her head. "We're like family now—or if not yet, we will be if Akash has anything to do with it."

"Oh no. We're just dating," Reena answered.

Asha narrowed her eyes at her. "You sure about that?" She nodded at something behind Reena. "I'll be in touch." She turned and hurried out of the office.

Akash watched his sister leave and Reena slowly turn around to face him. He had shoved nervous hands into his pockets and he was sure he was grinning like an idiot. "I have told you time and time again that this outfit looks better with diamonds."

She rolled her eyes at him. "I told you, I don't need diamond studs."

"We'll discuss that later. But I wasn't thinking *ear*rings." His heart thudded in his chest as he pulled the diamond ring from his pocket and held it out to her. He quickly closed the small distance between them.

Her eyes widened and glassed over with tears, but her smile was radiant. "Let me be yours," he said softly. "Forever."

"You already are."

She met his gaze as he slipped the ring on her finger. "And you always will be." Her hazel eyes never left his, not even to look at the ring. She leaned into him, wrapped her arms around his neck and kissed him like she belonged only to him.

Epilogue

Reena's Twenty-Eighth Birthday

"Shh. Hush. She'll hear you, Nila."

"You are standing on my foot, Kirti."

"Where's Sonny?"

"I'm right here."

"You guys are really bad at this whole surprise thing," Asha said.

"It's dark."

"That's the point."

"Family. She's on the elevator," James said quietly. "Do we have the paperwork?"

"Yes," said Akash. He held up the contract.

The lights flicked on and they all yelled at once. "SURPRISE!"

They all watched and cheered as Reena screamed in shock, then took a minute to catch her breath.

Reena's eyes widened as she took in her surroundings and all the people in the room. She searched until she found the dark eyes she wanted to see most. "Oh, you guys! Thank you."

It was her twenty-eighth birthday, and she was surrounded by everyone she loved.

In the meantime, James and Sonny began popping bottles of champagne to get ready for a toast. Akash cut through the crowd and approached her with papers. "Kirti has something to tell you." He turned to give her space.

"Reena Ben. Lulu's has made a profit."

Reena's eyes widened. "How much?"

"Enough for you to buy your two percent," Kirti said, and she looked at Akash.

Akash stepped forward again and placed the papers on her desk. "You sign here. And here, and someone from legal will come and show you the rest, but once you sign, you'll have fifty-one percent of Lulu's. She'll belong to you again." Akash's smile was so huge, her heart melted.

"This is amazing." Apparently, they were all going to watch her sign. She flipped through the papers until she got to the payment part. She picked up a pen and made a small adjustment.

Akash peeked over her shoulder. "What are you doing? I thought this was what you wanted. You worked so hard."

"This," she pointed to the new number, "is what I

want." She looked up at the family. Even her parents were here. "I will only be purchasing one percent. Then Akash and I will be equal partners. Fifty-fifty." She grinned up at him. "We both worked hard. And I love us being business partners. And friends. And fiancés. But we'll have to change the fiancé thing, don't you think?"

"Let's plan a wedding," he said.

"No."

"No?" He looked out at the families. They all had ridiculous grins on their faces.

"Already planned," Reena said. "Thanks to Sangeeta. Festivities start tonight."

Akash took her into his arms and pulled her close with everyone watching. "You're going to keep me on my toes."

"You can count on it," she whispered. "You going to kiss me or what?"

* * * * *

COMING NEXT MONTH FROM

(H) HARLEQUIN®
SPECIAL EDITION™

#2995 A MAVERICK REBORN
Montana Mavericks: Lassoing Love • by Melissa Senate
Handsome loner cowboy Bobby Stone has his issues--from faking his own death
three years ago to discovering a twin brother he never knew. But headstrong rodeo
queen Tori Hawkins is just the woman to break through his tough facade. First with
a rambunctious fling...and later with the healing love Bobby's always needed...

#2996 RANCHER TO THE RESCUE
Men of the West • by Stella Bagwell
Mack Barlow may have broken Dr. Grace Hollister's heart in high school, but sparks
still fly when the now-single father walks into her medical clinic. His young daughter
is adorable. And he's...too dang sexy by far! Can a very busy divorced mom take a
second chance on loving the man who once left her behind?

#2997 OLD DOGS, NEW TRUTHS
Sierra's Web • by Tara Taylor Quinn
When heiress Lindsay Warren-Smythe assumes a false identity to meet her
biological father, she's not expecting to develop a connection with her new
coworker, Cole Bennet, and his lovable dog. Cole has learned the hard way not to
trust beautiful liars with his heart, so when he lets his guard down with Lindsay, will
her lies tear them apart?

#2998 MATCHMAKER ON THE RANCH
Forever, Texas • by Marie Ferrarella
Rancher Chris Parnell has known Rosemary Robinson all his life. But working side
by side with the beautiful vet to diagnose the sickness affecting his cattle kicks him
completely out of his friend zone! Roe can't deny the attraction sizzling between
them. But will her friend with benefits stick around once the cattle mystery is solved?

#2999 HER YOUNGER MAN
Sutton's Place • by Shannon Stacey
Widow Laura Thompson falling for a younger man? Not on your life! Except
Riley Thompson is so dang charming. And handsome. And everything Laura's
missing in her life. The town seems to be against their romance. Including Riley's
boss...who's Laura's son! Are Riley and Laura strong enough to take a stand for love?

#3000 IN TOO DEEP
Love at Hideaway Wharf • by Laurel Greer
Chef Kellan Murphy is determined to fulfill his sister's dying wish. But placing an
ocean-fearing man in a scuba diving class is ridiculous! Instructor Sam Walker
can't resist helping the handsome wannabe diver overcome his fears. And their
unexpected connection is the perfect remedy for Sam's own hidden pain...

**YOU CAN FIND MORE INFORMATION ON UPCOMING HARLEQUIN TITLES,
FREE EXCERPTS AND MORE AT HARLEQUIN.COM.**

HSECNM0623

Get 3 FREE REWARDS!

We'll send you 2 FREE Books plus a FREE Mystery Gift.

FREE
Value Over
$20

Both the **Harlequin® Special Edition** and **Harlequin® Heartwarming™** series feature compelling novels filled with stories of love and strength where the bonds of friendship, family and community unite.

YES! Please send me 2 FREE novels from the Harlequin Special Edition or Harlequin Heartwarming series and my FREE Gift (gift is worth about $10 retail). After receiving them, if I don't wish to receive any more books, I can return the shipping statement marked "cancel." If I don't cancel, I will receive 6 brand-new Harlequin Special Edition books every month and be billed just $5.49 each in the U.S. or $6.24 each in Canada, a savings of at least 12% off the cover price, or 4 brand-new Harlequin Heartwarming Larger-Print books every month and be billed just $6.24 each in the U.S. or $6.74 each in Canada, a savings of at least 19% off the cover price. It's quite a bargain! Shipping and handling is just 50¢ per book in the U.S. and $1.25 per book in Canada.* I understand that accepting the 2 free books and gift places me under no obligation to buy anything. I can always return a shipment and cancel at any time by calling the number below. The free books and gift are mine to keep no matter what I decide.

Choose one: ☐ **Harlequin Special Edition** (235/335 BPA GRMK) ☐ **Harlequin Heartwarming Larger-Print** (161/361 BPA GRMK) ☐ **Or Try Both!** (235/335 & 161/361 BPA GRPZ)

Name (please print)

Address   Apt. #

City   State/Province   Zip/Postal Code

Email: Please check this box ☐ if you would like to receive newsletters and promotional emails from Harlequin Enterprises ULC and its affiliates. You can unsubscribe anytime.

Mail to the **Harlequin Reader Service:**
IN U.S.A.: P.O. Box 1341, Buffalo, NY 14240-8531
IN CANADA: P.O. Box 603, Fort Erie, Ontario L2A 5X3

Want to try 2 free books from another series! Call 1-800-873-8635 or visit www.ReaderService.com.

*Terms and prices subject to change without notice. Prices do not include sales taxes, which will be charged (if applicable) based on your state or country of residence. Canadian residents will be charged applicable taxes. Offer not valid in Quebec. This offer is limited to one order per household. Books received may not be as shown. Not valid for current subscribers to the Harlequin Special Edition or Harlequin Heartwarming series. All orders subject to approval. Credit or debit balances in a customer's account(s) may be offset by any other outstanding balance owed by or to the customer. Please allow 4 to 6 weeks for delivery. Offer available while quantities last.

Your Privacy—Your information is being collected by Harlequin Enterprises ULC, operating as Harlequin Reader Service. For a complete summary of the information we collect, how we use this information and to whom it is disclosed, please visit our privacy notice located at corporate.harlequin.com/privacy-notice. From time to time we may also exchange your personal information with reputable third parties. If you wish to opt out of this sharing of your personal information, please visit readerservice.com/consumerschoice or call 1-800-873-8635. **Notice to California Residents**—Under California law, you have specific rights to control and access your data. For more information on these rights and how to exercise them, visit corporate.harlequin.com/california-privacy.

HSEHW23

HARLEQUIN
PLUS

Try the best multimedia subscription service for romance readers like you!

Read, Watch and Play.

Experience the easiest way to get the romance content you crave.

Start your **FREE TRIAL** at
www.harlequinplus.com/freetrial.